In Love with the Wrong Man

Scandalous Sheiks

Elizabeth Lennox

Table of Contents

Chapter 1

"Relax!" Sandoor teased. "He's going to love you!"

Maya tried to smile, but her blue eyes were wide as Sandoor led her into the shockingly huge and elegant palace. "I just...he's your older brother, so I want to make a good impression." Maya nervously smoothed her hands over her yellow sundress, hoping it wasn't too wrinkled from traveling. "It was a long flight and I'm sure I'm a complete mess. Maybe we should...?"

Sandoor laughed, throwing an arm around her shoulders and pulling her in for a hug. "You look beautiful, as always," he assured her. His dark, teasing eyes glanced down, his mouth pulling into a grimace. "Although, that stain on your dress might..."

Maya gasped and jerked away as she peered down at her dress. "Oh no! Where? What did I...?"

He chuckled again, pulling her back against his side, kissing her forehead. "Just kidding!"

Maya groaned, and lightly elbowed him before they continued forward. "You're horrible!" she grumbled.

"I know," he replied, not at all offended. "But you love me anyway."

Maya rolled her eyes. "Right now, I'm not so sure I do."

His grin was contagious, as always. "Hey, at least now you're not terrified of meeting my brother!" he offered.

Her eyes widened again at the reminder and she turned away from Sandoor, her anxiety ramping up as she searched the long hallway for the mysterious brother. "Thanks for reminding me."

Sandoor laughed and Maya ignored him. He was a horrible tease, but that was one of the many reasons she loved him so much. Sandoor was fun and outgoing, urging her to do things that she normally would shy away from. Like traveling halfway around the world to meet the

1

incredibly intimidating Sheik Jahlil bin Asdoor, ruler of Celina.

"Don't worry so much," Sandoor soothed, his voice turning serious. "Jahlil is going to love you, just as I do."

Maya wasn't convinced, but she continued down the long, elaborately decorated hallway towards the administrative offices of the palace. She didn't like being here, but since she was engaged to Sandoor, she needed to get over her fears. She toyed with the heavy diamond ring on her finger. It was too big and gaudy for her tastes, but she knew that Sandoor loved flashy things. Because she loved Sandoor, she would learn to love the ring. Eventually. She hoped.

A moment later, she felt Sandoor squeeze her arm. "Want to take a detour and explore the stables first?"

Maya shot him a glare. "I thought your brother was expecting us?"

He shrugged which drew her admiring gaze to his broad shoulders. "He is. But I don't want you to be nervous. This is supposed to be a fun visit!"

Maya tamped down her irritation at his casual dismissal of this meeting with his older brother. Sandoor loved having fun and consistently avoided stressful situations, which annoyed Maya at times. But as soon as the thought popped into her head, she stopped it in its tracks. She loved Sandoor and needed to accept him the way he was. If he was wildly irresponsible at times, Maya had to accept that. She loved him no matter what. And besides, wasn't his fun-loving nature part of the reason she'd accepted his proposal? Maya knew that she was too serious most of the time. Sandoor pulled her out of her shell, got her away from the library, and taught her how to live a little.

"Sandoor!"

Maya jumped, startled by the voice booming down the hallway. Turning, she looked around, then gasped involuntarily when she saw the man walking towards them. Sandoor was tall, but this guy...! He was a giant! He was a linebacker! But with more muscles and an expression that whispered that this man didn't know the meaning of the word "fun"!

Maya's body went cold, then hot when she felt this man's dark eyes focus on her. Something inside of her tightened as he walked towards them! She felt...a humming inside of her. No, that wasn't right. It was more of a...? She couldn't think. Maya had never experienced anything like this and her mind simply refused to define her reaction.

Her eyes drank in every detail as he approached, and yet, her mind was still completely blank. The rest of the world faded away. She couldn't see the servants rushing around. The elaborate tapestries and all of the beautiful mosaics faded away. It was just this man, his sharp nose and angular cheekbones, hard jawline and uncompromising mouth.

She felt an odd tremor bolt through her. Every cell within her seemed to tremble with awareness. Those dark, impenetrable eyes should have been warm and comforting, but the sharp gaze seemed to move down her figure, slowly taking in every detail. Maya was vaguely aware of her breasts tingling with his intense perusal, but she couldn't seem to move. She was like a rabbit caught by the lion's gaze!

"Jahlil!"

Maya blinked and finally managed to turn to Sandoor, who was grinning happily as the enormous man approached. Then Sandoor rushed forward, leaving her standing awkwardly in the wide hallway! The giant wrapped massive arms around Sandoor's more slender frame. Then Sandoor laughed? How was that possible? Of course, Sandoor laughed at everything! But Maya didn't understand his amusement. It seemed wrong. Out of place.

Sandoor stepped back, still beaming up at his brother, but his body turned. That's when the lion's eyes focused on Maya. Her heart tried to leap clear out of her chest, her skin felt cold and clammy, then a wave of heat rolled over her. His eyes...somehow both intimidating and inviting. How was that even possible?

"Who is your friend?" he asked.

Sandoor laughed, wrapping an arm around her waist. "Jahlil, I'd like to introduce you to Maya Tisdale," he said with a great deal of pride in his voice.

There was a horrible moment when Maya thought to stop Sandoor from announcing their engagement. The spark of doubt hit her like a gut punch. She actually had to restrain herself from slapping a hand over Sandoor's mouth. She struggled to remain calm, despite the sick sensation pooling in her stomach.

But Sandoor continued, blithely unaware of her panic, "She has graciously agreed to be my wife!"

Maya watched Jahlil, noticed his eyes narrow ever so slightly. Her heart thudded and for a moment, she felt shame! Then Sandoor's sweet smile came into her view and she forced herself to relax.

"I told you that he wasn't an ogre!" Sandoor announced, still laughing. Because everything was a joke to Sandoor, Maya thought, suppressing the flash of irritation. Again.

"It is a pleasure to meet you," Maya said, extending her hand. Not because she wanted to. But because it was the polite thing to do. Fighting her instincts to run and hide, she nervously waited for the man's reaction.

"Ms. Tisdale," the giant said, bowing slightly while, at the same time, enveloping her small hand in his giant paw. His fingers were hot as they surrounded hers and Maya wondered what it would be like to have this man's arms around her. Would he be gentle? Or rough? A shiver went through her at the possibility of both options. She knew that he felt that shiver because his hand tightened around hers and his dark eyes sharpened ever so slightly.

And then his warmth vanished. Maya blinked, surprised all over again as he pulled back. She wanted to scream at him to come back to her. But then Sandoor threw his arm over her shoulder. Once again, Sandoor was laughing at....whatever it was that he found hilarious. Maya peered up at Sandoor, trying to understand.

"Isn't she great?" he asked.

The giant pulled his eyes away, looking at his brother. "You mentioned bringing home a special friend," Jahlil said, his voice still deep and compelling. "I wasn't expecting..." he stopped, his gaze once again moving over Maya. "I apologize," he said, obviously changing his mind about explaining his expectations. Instead, the large man bowed slightly. "Welcome. I'll have someone show you to your rooms.

Maya frowned slightly. There were definitely some unspoken questions floating around right now. She glanced up at Sandoor and noticed the awkward expression, his clenched jaw. His arm suddenly tightened around her shoulders.

Maya was also struck by the similarities between the pair. Both were tall, although Jahlil topped Sandoor by several inches. Both men had similar coloring, although, on Sandoor, his dark hair and dark eyes looked cute and adorable. On the other man, those same features appeared...menacing.

Maya felt the sudden stress and needed to ease the tension between the brothers. "Your Highness, I appreciate–"

The man's eyes sharpened again and he held up a hand. "You're family now," he said. "You must call me Jahlil." There was a small pause and he glanced at Sandoor, then back at Maya. "Please, if you don't mind, I need to have a private word with my brother."

Maya couldn't decipher the strange undercurrents between the brothers. So instead, she nodded politely, trying to hide her relief at the opportunity to escape. "Of course. I'll just..." she wasn't sure what to do. The palace was enormous and she had no idea where to go in order to give these two men some privacy.

Thankfully, another man stepped forward. He looked very official, but also kind and friendly. "If you would follow me, Ms. Tisdale, I'll show you to your suite."

Maya released the breath she hadn't realized she'd been holding. "Thank you!" she almost gushed, eager to get away from the strange tension between the brothers.

Jahlil watched as the beautiful woman followed Tinar down the hallway. She was lovely, with obvious intelligence in her eyes, which warned him she wouldn't be easily fooled.

Which was why, once she was safely out of earshot, he said, "I wasn't expecting someone like her," he began, choosing his words with care.

Sandoor turned an interesting shade of pink. "She's pretty wonderful. She graduated at the top of her class in computer science at MIT."

"Ah," Jahlil nodded, waving his brother into his office. "So you met in Boston?"

Sandoor laughed. "Yes! She was in a coffee shop, studying. I'd seen her several times over several weeks. But she was always studying. I'd never seen her just relaxing or enjoying herself."

Jahlil closed the door to his office while Sandoor walked over to fill two crystal glasses with scotch. "And you decided that she needed a break from the studying?" he offered, knowing his brother extremely well. There was a nervousness in his movements that whispered to Jahlil that something wasn't right. Sandoor was an inherently honest and open person. So what was going on now? Why was Sandoor pouring scotch at nine o'clock in the morning?

"Exactly," Sandoor replied, still grinning a little too hard as he handed one of the glasses to Jahlil. "Maya is always so serious." He sat down in one of the leather chairs. "I considered it my responsibility to get her to loosen up."

Jahlil stared at his brother, trying to hide from the fact that he was still reeling from his encounter with the most beautiful, compelling woman he'd ever met. In other circumstances, Jahlil might wonder if this feeling was jealousy. But he adored Sandoor. Jahlil absolutely refused to be jealous of his little brother.

Still, Jahlil had thought...had always assumed that Sandoor...well, perhaps those assumptions were wrong. "I'm just..." he chose his words carefully, "surprised, actually."

Sandoor downed half of his scotch, balancing the glass on his knee. "Why would you be surprised?"

"Ms. Tisdale is...not what I was expecting," Jahlil replied. "She's beautiful," he said honestly. "But I just thought..." he sighed, rubbing his forehead. "Well, never mind what I thought." He lifted his glass in salute. "To your engagement!"

Sandoor laughed. Sandoor always laughed. To him, life was one continuous joke. He never took anything seriously. "So Ms. Tisdale is finished with her education?"

Sandoor rolled his eyes. "Don't start," he groaned.

"Don't start what?" Jahlil prompted, setting his glass of scotch down on the table. It was too early to start drinking and the fact that Sandoor had poured two glasses, almost automatically, was a bit worrisome. Scotch in the morning wasn't really his thing, but it seemed as if it was for his little brother. Jahlil watched as Sandoor downed the rest of his scotch, then stood up to pour himself more. A double this time.

"I know what you're thinking," Sandoor said, taking a long sip.

At least it was a sip this time, Jahlil thought, eyeing his younger brother carefully.

"I doubt it," Jahlil replied. At least, he hoped that his little brother didn't know what thoughts flitted through his mind.

"You're wondering when I'm going to buckle down and finish my degree," Sandoor said, waving his glass of scotch in the air like a salute. "And you're right. I need to buckle down and start studying. That's one of the things that's so great about Maya. She forces me to study."

Another point in her favor, Jahlil thought. "And when is the blessed event going to take place?" Jahlil asked, his tone more sarcastic than he'd intended. It was difficult though, listening to his little brother talk about school. He'd been attending classes at Harvard off and on for six years. The school had just sent a note explaining that Sandoor would be expelled if he didn't raise his grades to a more acceptable level. But Jahlil doubted his younger brother was ready for the usual 'get serious and get to work' speech. Besides, it hadn't changed Sandoor's behavior in the past. Why would it make a difference now?

"Maya said she won't marry me until I finish my degree," he laughed, slapping his knee as if that were the most hilarious thing in the world. "Isn't that great?"

Jahlil was silently impressed. The woman clearly wasn't an idiot. "That's wise."

Sandoor nodded, his features smoothing into a more serious expression. "She's good for me, Jahlil. She forces me to study. She's sweet, kind, and incredibly generous! She volunteers at the local homeless shelter, she crochets winter hats for people whenever she's not studying and she's so damn smart!" He leaned forward, looking into Jahlil's eyes. "She makes me want to be a better person, Jahlil. She's perfect for me!"

Jahlil nodded his head in agreement. He liked the sound of Maya better and better. If there was another spark of something strange, he ignored it. "That's good. So the wedding won't be for a while then?"

Sandoor sighed. "Exactly. I've changed majors so many times, I don't have enough credits to go toward any specific degree."

That was basically what the school had hinted at in the letter, but since Sandoor was saying it, Jahlil didn't bother mentioning the warning from Harvard. "Do you have a goal in mind now?"

"Maya thinks I should study business or political science. She says those subjects will help me with my responsibilities here." He looked a bit sheepish as he added, "Maya thinks I should figure out how I can best help you."

Jahlil's eyebrows lifted. "And you want to come back? Be a part of the government?" That was definitely good news!

"Well, at first, I didn't want to," Sandoor admitted. "I suggested that we could get a house in Los Angeles or maybe Manhattan." He laughed, shaking his head. "I told her about all of the fun stuff we could do." He leaned back in his chair. "I love the theater and I've dragged Maya to several performances. She enjoys it too, but not as much as I do." He sighed, looking a bit more resigned now. "But Maya gets this look about her when she disapproves," he explained, chuckling as he shook his head. "Anyway, she convinced me that I should face up to my responsibilities, or stop accepting money from you. She said that I shouldn't have the wealth that my title provides me if I'm unwilling to do the work that my title requires." He sighed, then finished off his second glass of scotch. "Which is why I'm here, Big Bro!" he exclaimed cheerfully. "I'm going to learn the family business!"

Jahlil cringed inwardly. "That's a very…" he paused, not sure what to say. "Well, that's incredibly generous of you, Sandoor." Jahlil mentally sifted through his list of projects currently under way within the government, wondering which would suit Sandoor's personality. Jahlil adored his brother, but Sandoor was a bit…well, he wasn't the most responsible member of the royal family.

"I thought so too!" he replied, thinking that was hilariously funny. He leaned forward. "One thing though. I know that I brought Maya here to meet you, and I really hope that you two get to know each other. But the thing is," he paused, standing up to pour himself a third scotch. He took a long swallow before he continued. "The thing is - Mike," he stopped and took another sip. "You remember my friend, Mike? I've told you about him before." He paused barely long enough for Jahlil to nod. "Well, Mike is getting a group of guys together for a climbing trip. I thought it would be a good last hurrah before I settle down and finish my degree. I figure it will take me another two years, give or take, before I'm able to finish my degree."

Jahlil wasn't sure how to respond. "A climbing trip?" he prompted.

"With Mike? You've mentioned Mike several times over the past few months." Jahlil watched, fascinated as his younger brother blushed and looked hastily away.

Sandoor's fingers tightened around the now empty glass. "Yeah, Mike is a good guy."

Leaning forward, Jahlil looked into Sandoor's eyes. "I'd love to meet him some day. Would you consider bringing *him* home when you have a chance?" he asked, trying to convey that Jahlil supported his younger brother, no matter what. Sandoor was a happy-go-lucky guy. Or at least, Jahlil had thought so, but the excessive drinking was new and rather worrisome. And this Mike guy...Jahlil had gotten the impression there was something special going on between Mike and his brother. Was he wrong?

The blush that stole up Sandoor's neck proved that Jahlil wasn't off the mark. This Mike guy...he was special to Sandoor. So, why was Maya here? What was going on? Why was Sandoor engaged to Maya when his brother clearly had feelings for Mike?!

"Mike is engaged to a lovely woman," Sandoor said, toying with his glass. "They will be married in about two months."

"Ah!" Jahlil replied, understanding dawning. "Is *that* why you proposed to Maya then?"

Sandoor's eyes lifted, and the raw pain in his brother's gaze startled Jahlil. He opened his mouth to say something, then shook his head slightly. "No. Of course not." Sandoor thought for another moment, then shrugged. "I love Maya. She's great. And she's good for me."

Jahlil didn't comment as he considered everything that had been said. And what hadn't been said, which was probably more important. Finally, he nodded his head. "That's good to hear. One's life partner should balance out one's personality."

Sandoor's troubled features morphed back into his customary grin. "That's what I said when Maya turned down my proposals the first few times." He chuckled, shaking his head at the memories. "She kept saying that we're too different. That we might work out in the short term, but long term, we'd grow to hate each other." He laughed again. "But I said that we balance each other. We're two extremes. She's all serious and sedate while I'm more extravagant and frivolous. I convinced her that she needed me in her life to give her laughter and adventure."

"Like rock climbing?" Jahlil offered, more impressed with Maya now that he knew more about the relationship. He was still confused though.

"Yeah," Sandoor replied, and turned serious again. He glanced down at his shoes, at his empty glass of scotch, then finally lifted his eyes to look beseechingly at Jahlil. "I was hoping that...well, maybe you could keep an eye on Maya for me? Make sure that she's okay while I'm gone?"

What the hell? Sandoor was leaving his fiancée, basically abandoning her in a foreign country surrounded by strangers? Namely, himself? His eyes sharpened as he frowned at his brother. "You're not taking her with you?"

He slapped his knee as he laughed at the possibility. "Maya? On a mountain? Oh hell no! She doesn't even like climbing ladders!"

Jahlil's eyebrow lifted at that. "So, when are you going on this 'last hurrah'?"

Sandoor shuffled his feet uncomfortably. "Mike was finally able to get some time off this weekend. Do you think...?"

"That's in two days!" Jahlil snapped, tamping down firmly on the sudden urge to shake his brother. "You came here to introduce me to your fiancée, and you're going to abandon her so that you can take a climbing trip?"

Sandoor shrugged, looking a bit worried now. "Well, it all came together so quickly. The opening with the climbing team wasn't expected. And I know how tight your schedule is. So when you told me that you had time this weekend to meet someone special, I got Maya on the plane as fast as I could. I didn't want to lose this opportunity for the two of you to meet."

Jahlil was trying to understand the subtexts here, but for once, Sandoor wasn't being his normal, straightforward self. Which, in itself, was strange. Sandoor was usually an open book. He was a fun-loving man-child that always knew where to find a group of people to hang out with, always knew where the fun was. He could sniff out a good time anywhere, or he'd create a good time by gathering like-minded people around him. Jahlil didn't condemn his younger brother because of Sandoor's need for adventure. He accepted him for who he was. But leaving Maya in a couple of days with strangers? That didn't bode well for a happy life together.

Jahlil had thought that he'd understood and respected Sandoor. Now he wasn't so sure.

And yet, Jahlil knew that there was no way to convince Sandoor that abandoning his fiancée was a bad idea. So instead, he nodded and agreed to Sandoor's request. "Maya is family now. Of course I'll watch out for her," Jahlil assured his younger brother. "How long will this trip be?"

Sandoor's shoulders dropped and his tight features relaxed back into an easy grin. "Just three days. I want to collect Maya before I register for classes in Boston. We're on a tight schedule, since she's starting her new job in about two weeks and needs to pack up her apartment. She's moving to a new place, one a bit further away from campus, but much more affordable."

This was a surprise. "You won't be living together?" he asked, impressed all over again by the woman's choices.

Sandoor flushed as he shook his head. "No. Maya told me that I have to prove myself before she'll move in with me. She also wants to prove something to herself. She wants to live on her own to prove to herself that she can make it on her own in the world. She's very ambitious and is eager to start her new job." He grinned, bowing his head slightly. "She's going to be amazing at it too!"

Jahlil nodded, thinking that Maya was indeed a very interesting woman. Smart, beautiful, and she'd caught the attention of Sandoor. She must be a good person!

"That's very sensible of her," Jahlil said, thinking of how pretty her blue eyes were and the way her lips had trembled when he'd shaken her hand. "Let me know what I can do to help."

Jahlil stood up, taking Sandoor's glass and setting it on the table, hoping that his brother didn't help himself to any more. Already, Sandoor's eyes were a bit glassy. "You must be exhausted from your trip. Why don't you go relax by the pool?" he offered.

Sandoor smiled, nodding in agreement. "Yeah, that sounds nice." He started to leave, then turned back. "Thanks," he said, his voice filled with sincerity. "You've always supported me, Jahlil." For a moment, he looked defeated. "I know I'm a mess. Maya has talked to me about taking on more responsibility, to stop acting so silly."

Jahlil's eyes sharpened. "She said that to you?" Angry on Sandoor's behalf.

Sandoor laughed. "No way! She used pretty words, just like you. But I still got the message." He smiled sadly. "Maya said basically the same thing that you've been trying to tell me this whole time. That I need to grow up." He sighed, rubbing his hands over his slacks. "Maya is going to help me do that. It's going to be different. You'll see," he vowed. "From now on, as soon as I get back from this trip, I'll be a different man. Someone that you and Maya can be proud of."

And with that, he left Jahlil's office with his chin held high.

Jahlil blinked at the now-closed door, wondering just what the lovely Maya had said to Sandoor. Whatever it was, Jahlil appreciated her efforts. He also appreciated the fact that they weren't jumping into marriage immediately. Still, the engagement seemed sudden. Jahlil called his younger brother at least once a week, just to check in and chat. Of course, Sandoor's body guards also submitted reports of his activities, but no one had mentioned this Maya person. At least, he didn't think so. Perhaps he should go back through the reports. In previous weeks, Jahlil had read through the reports looking for news of Mike. Not someone with a female name.

  Time to dig a bit deeper into Maya's background. He was pretty sure that the beautiful Maya was hiding something behind those big, blue eyes of hers.

Chapter 2

"Can I help you?"

Maya jumped, startled, covering her mouth to keep herself from screaming. When she saw the large shadow, she froze. But as the huge shadow unfolded, Maya recognized Sheik Jahlil Bin Asdoor. "Your Highness!" she murmured nervously. "I'm so sorry. I didn't mean to disturb you." She started to back away, but the deep voice that had kept her awake most of the night stopped her retreat.

"Don't go," he commanded. There was something so authoritative about that voice. She stopped and turned around, watching as he came nearer, his shadow dancing in and out of the moonlight coming in through the windows. "It's two o'clock in the morning. What are you doing up and about?"

"I just…" she sighed, tucking her hair behind her ears, painfully conscious of the fact that she wasn't wearing a bra. She'd gone to sleep in just an old tee-shirt and panties. When the hours had ticked by and she knew that she wasn't going to get to sleep without a little help, she'd pulled on a pair of loose shorts. She prayed that he couldn't see her too clearly in the dim light. "I often have trouble sleeping."

"And you decided that wandering around the palace would help?"

She felt her cheeks heat up and was grateful for the lack of bright lights. "I was looking for the kitchen. Warm milk usually helps me to fall asleep," she explained awkwardly. When he continued to stare down at her, she clenched her fingers together. "Milk has small amounts of tryptophan, which is the precursor to serotonin. Although, not really enough to induce sleep, it seems to help." She tried to stop rambling, but her tongue refused to give control back to her brain. When she was nervous, she chattered, she couldn't seem to stop. "It isn't necessarily the tryptophan that helps me sleep." She crossed her arms over her stomach, then forced herself to drop them back at her sides, worried that the gesture made her look defensive. "The proteins in the milk actually inhibit the absorption of the tryptophan. One would need to eat more carbohydrates to help the brain process such a small amount of the chemical and..." she trailed off, grasping that he was struggling not to laugh at her. "Well, it helps," she finished lamely and sighed.

"You went the wrong way. The kitchen is that way." He turned and pointed.

She frowned and looked around. "I did? But...I thought..." she stared into the darkness, but she didn't recognize this hallway. Sighing, she lifted her hands into the air helplessly, and let them drop. "I have no idea where I am."

He laughed and Maya thought the sound was...unsettling in an odd way.

"This way," he said, waving at her to follow, turning down the hallway in the other direction.

"Oh!" she turned, starting to follow him. "You don't have to..." she stopped because he was already striding off down the hallway. She hurried to catch up, painfully aware that she should have put on more clothes before venturing out of her suite. "If you just tell me how to get there, I can find it myself."

He glanced at her as she quickened her pace. "We'd find you wandering the stables tomorrow morning if I don't show you the way," he teased.

She laughed nervously. Had his gaze darted down to her breasts? She certainly hoped not. Sandoor was always very sweet about not noticing when she was less than perfectly dressed. In fact, that was one of the things that she liked about him. Maya knew that she could just be herself, as casual as she liked and Sandoor would just...accept it. She never felt any pressure from him in any way.

"What is keeping you awake?" he asked, pushing through a set of double doors. They continued down another long hallway, this one less fancy than the previous area.

"I just...I guess I'm still on Boston time. Right now it's..." she blinked, trying to calculate the time difference.

"Seven o'clock in the morning," he supplied, without skipping a beat.

Seven? But...then why did she feel so tired?

"Dehydration," he added, seeming to read her mind. "The air on a plane is extremely dry. They take as much of the humidity out of the air as possible to keep the weight of the plane down," he explained, pausing outside of another set of double doors. "You need to drink more water when flying. Otherwise, your mind and body are thrown out of balance. Add in the fact that we're in a desert…" He shrugged and eyed her meaningfully.

"Is that right?" she asked, even though she'd read that somewhere. "I guess I just need some water then."

He pushed through the doors, revealing a spacious kitchen. "I'll warm you up some milk, just to ensure that you can get some rest tonight."

He walked over to one of several large refrigerators, the steel kind that commercial restaurants used. Reaching in, he took out a jug of milk and carried it over to the stove, then moved to a rack of pans hanging down from hooks high up over a steel counter.

"You don't have to do that for me," she exclaimed. "I'm sure that you have more important things to do. Maybe you could use some sleep yourself?" she teased.

He laughed softly, turning the heat on under the pan.

"I'm fine," he replied.

She stared at him for a moment, noticing the tension in his jaw. "You have trouble sleeping too, don't you?"

He shrugged noncommittally as he poured milk into the pan. "What's on your mind?" he asked, grabbing a metal stool and bringing it over to the counter, pointing to it as if telling her to sit. She sat.

"I just…I've always had trouble sleeping. I remember sneaking into the family room as a kid so that I could sleep on the couch." She shrugged. "For some reason, it was easier to sleep on the couch than in my bed."

Jahlil grabbed a wooden spoon, stirring thoughtfully before asking, "What was your room like as a child?"

"White," she replied. "White walls, white bedspread, white furniture, and white pillows. But I had lots of stuffed animals. I used to pile them up on the bed. I loved the bright colors." She eyed him curiously, the strong muscles along his back and arms flexing appealingly as he stirred the milk. "What's on your mind?"

He turned his head and she saw the surprise in his eyes. Had no one ever asked him what bothered him? Probably not, she thought. Jahlil looked as if he could take on the world, and have strength left over to start working on the rest of the solar system. But she saw it. In his eyes, there was surprise. Yes, things bothered him. Deeply, she thought with surprise.

"I had some reports to read," he explained.

There was a long silence and Maya considered his words. And what he wasn't saying. "And the information in those reports bothered you?"

Another startled look. "Yes."

She shifted slightly, leaning forward on her elbows. "Sometimes it helps to talk about it."

He continued to stare at the milk. "I can handle it," he said.

"I'm sure you can." She sighed. "Okay, so I'm guessing that the bothersome reports are top secret and you can't talk about them. So, why don't you talk about something else?" she offered. When he looked at her with a dark eyebrow lifted with amusement, she shrugged. "Sometimes it helps me to talk about something else. Then my brain isn't so focused on the bad stuff. I'm concentrating on the good stuff. So tell me something good, Your Highness."

He smiled slightly. Well, it wasn't a smile so much as a crooked lift of his chiseled mouth. She waited, her breath caught in her throat, hoping that he might reveal a little bit about himself. Why was this revelation, this moment in time, so important? Maya had no idea. But watching him, she knew that she was fascinated. As she should be! It wasn't a bad thing to be concerned. He would be her brother-in-law very soon.

Well, not all that soon, she mentally corrected. She'd told Sandoor that she wouldn't marry him until he finished school and she was going to stick to that vow. At his current pace, he wouldn't finish for another decade.

Maybe he'd come to his senses by then.

Woah! Where had that thought come from? Maya blinked, startled by the thought. She loved Sandoor. Didn't she?

Yes. But enough for marriage?

Hmm...now, that was the big question.

When she looked back at Jahlil, she noticed that he'd been watching her. Quickly, she hid her fears behind what she hoped was a bland smile.

"You're stalling," she teased. "Tell me something that isn't upsetting."

Those hard lips twitched again and Maya felt a surge of triumph. Because she was helping him relax? She made Sandoor laugh all the time! Of course, Sandoor laughed no matter what was happening. For some reason, helping Jahlil, and yes, she was beginning to think of him by his first name, to relax, would be a pretty wonderful accomplishment.

Jahlil stirred the milk without really seeing it. Instead, his mind replayed the soft, gentle concern in Maya's eyes. She was incredibly sweet, he thought. The very idea that he could talk about something non-controversial in order to push away the bad thoughts was an astounding and naïve thought. It was also sweet that she wanted to help to get his mind off the reports he'd just read. They were pretty horrific, and the consequences of the decisions he needed to make were...either decision he made...would hurt someone. Her efforts wouldn't work, but for some reason, he searched his memory for something to tell her. Something that she might like.

"The daughter of one of my generals just gave birth to a little girl." Now where the hell had that come from? He remembered walking into a meeting today and hearing General Azari bragging about his new granddaughter. But as soon as Jahlil had walked in, the room went quiet and everyone quickly took their seats, beginning the briefing on a military base that had seen more threats than normal lately. The general had given a report on how the base commander was dealing with the threats, then they'd moved on to other potential problems.

"That's wonderful!" she gasped, wiggling slightly with excitement. He noticed the way her breasts swayed gently under her thin shirt and braced himself.

"Seven pounds, eight ounces," he recited. What did it matter how much the baby weighed? It was a mystery why anyone would talk about a baby's weight. It wasn't as if the child's weight would ever come up again. But for some reason, a birth weight was significant. "Ten toes and ten fingers too," he added. He thought about the pride on General Aziri's face when he'd relayed that news. He'd been over the moon with excitement.

"What is her name?" Maya asked eagerly.

Jahlil took a mug down off of one of the shelves. This wasn't a mug that any of his staff would serve to him. But it looked sturdy enough for the job. He poured the warm milk into the mug, and added a bit of sugar and a sprinkle of nutmeg.

"I don't know, actually," he replied, setting the mug down in front of her.

She blinked at the mug and looked up at him. "Aren't you going to join me?" she asked.

He eyed the steaming milk, then shrugged. "I'm not necessarily a fan of milk," he told her, trying, and failing, to hide his amusement.

"I guess not. You're the strong manly-man type. Obviously, drinking warm milk would ruin your rugged image, wouldn't it?"

She hid her laughter behind the mug as she watched him.

Jahlil rolled his eyes, but because she'd dared him, he snagged another mug from the shelf. With resignation, he poured the rest of the milk into the cup, and added a bit of sugar and nutmeg. Not that he was going to drink the foul stuff. But he'd humor her, if only because she was his future sister-in-law.

Sitting down, he stared at her across the expanse of the counter. "Satisfied?" he asked, glaring at her with mock severity.

"Absolutely. Okay, so your general has a new granddaughter. What is he like? Will he be a good grandfather?"

Jahlil thought about it. "I suppose so. What makes a man a good grandfather?"

She shrugged and his gaze once again dropped to her breasts. Sister-in-law, he repeated, mentally giving himself a shake. Completely, irrevocably, off limits!

"Oh, I don't know. I guess the requirements are similar to being a good parent. Someone who will love their child or grandchild without reservation. Someone strong enough to say no, when appropriate. But soft enough to say yes whenever possible. I think there should be more yeses from grandparents," she said with a smile. "Parents have to be the bossy ones since they have to set boundaries, while grandparents are allowed," she tilted her head thoughtfully, "no, not just allowed, but perhaps even required, to spoil grandchildren whenever possible and within a parent's limits."

He thought about that for a moment, before nodding. "Then yes, I think that Aziri will be an excellent grandfather. And his wife is very sweet and kind. She loves to bake. Aziri regularly brings in pastries or cookies his wife baked. So, I guess she'll make a good grandmother."

Her fingers were long and slender, he noticed. She cupped the ceramic mug in the palms of her hands and he wondered what it would be like to feel those soft fingers on his...*sister-in-law*!

"That sort of gives one hope for the world, doesn't it?"

Her smile distracted him. It took him a moment to focus on her eyes. "What do you mean?" He thought about the soldier who was captured last week on a secret mission that he'd signed off on. The man might die in the next few hours. Or the ship that he'd authorized to enter enemy territory, simply as a precaution because a Brumadi warship was inching closer to Celina waters. Sailors on both ships were in danger if tensions escalated. At this point, anything could happen and everyone was braced for...for something potentially horrible.

"I don't know," she sighed, taking a sip of her milk. "There are so many bad things happening in the world. Robberies, murders, and car crashes."

"And this gives you hope?" he teased.

She laughed, but turned serious. "No, that doesn't give me hope. It's the fact that, despite all of that, people are still falling in love. Couples have enough faith in the world that they are willing to bring a new child into it." She tilted her head slightly. "Did you know that economists calculate the arrival of a recession based partly on the birth rate?"

"You don't say?" he teased.

She smiled, those long, dark lashes lowering to hood her beautiful eyes. "Right. You probably know all about this."

"Not the birth rate issue," he admitted easily. "What do you mean?"

She leaned forward and, this time, he managed to keep his eyes on her face. Barely.

"Well, they don't know exactly why, but sociologists and economists are starting to see a pattern in the way the general population perceives something that isn't currently showing up in the data. Employees around the world, and in all types of industries, have a sort of sixth sense about the future, whether it is positive or negative. People somehow know, unconsciously, that an economic downturn is on the horizon and they are less likely to decide to get pregnant."

He hadn't heard that before, but it made sense. "So the fact that people are still having babies means that the economy is going to be good?"

"Well, not exactly," she laughed. "It isn't that simple. You have to look ahead. How many babies are on the way, so to speak? What's the trend versus the big picture at the moment? That's how they anticipate economic issues in the future."

He nodded his head. "But babies right now give you hope?"

"Yes. Anytime a new baby is born, I feel a surge of hope and optimism. It doesn't have to be a human baby. I love kittens and puppies and all sorts of animals!" She laughed softly, turning slightly on the stool. "I remember that one of the zoos in the United States had a giraffe that was about to give birth. But they weren't sure when, exactly, it would happen." She smiled, rolling her eyes. "You'd think the veterinarians would know how to predict when a giraffe was going to give birth. I mean, didn't they..." she stopped, blushing, but Jahlil saw her determination as she continued with her story, "they impregnated the giraffe, I suspect." If the lights weren't so dim, Jahlil suspected he would see her blushing. "Anyway, the expectant-momma giraffe was walking around in her enclosure, and they had a live feed watching her all the time. People from all over the world tuned in for this live stream where nothing happened other than the momma giraffe walking around, eating, and sometimes making noises."

"What happened?" he asked, thinking he vaguely remembered the story.

"Nothing!" she laughed. "Nothing at all! For weeks, this giraffe, I think her name was April, just endured her pregnancy. But millions of people regularly tuned in, hoping and cheering for her."

"It sounds...boring," he replied.

Maya laughed and nodding. "It was. But that's not the point."

"What was the point?" he teased, enjoying her animation.

"The point is, there was hope. Hope for the mother giraffe. Hope that her seemingly unending pregnancy would finally end. Hope that the baby giraffe would be healthy." She sighed. "Just hope. That's the point."

He nodded, and looked down, surprised to find the warm milk in his mug had vanished. When had he drunk the milk?

"It's an interesting theory, at least," she said, standing up and yawning. He watched as she took his mug and walked over to the sink, filling both up with water and setting them down in the sink. His eyes moved to her derriere, impressed with the round curves. Nice, although he had to admit, if only to himself, that he was more of a breast or leg man.

Then his eyes dropped to her legs. They were strong and smooth, tanned from whatever she did outside. And they were gorgeous!

Ripping his eyes away, he again reminded himself that Maya was his future sister-in-law. He shouldn't be looking at her legs. He shouldn't be thinking about her legs!

"Okay, well, thank you for sharing milk and conversation with me," she said as she turned around. "I think I'll be able to sleep now." She smiled shyly up at him. "Good night."

Then she was gone. Jahlil stared at the doorway through which she'd disappeared, wishing that she'd come back and keep talking with him. He had about another two hours of work to read through and he didn't want to deal with it. Was his younger brother's irresponsibility rubbing off on him?

He looked at the time. Hell, it was well past three o'clock in the morning. He had to be up early for a briefing on...something. He didn't remember the topic just now. So, instead of turning to the left to go back to his office, he turned to the right. He'd read the last few reports in bed, he decided.

But as soon as he reached his room, he stripped off his clothes and headed for bed. He'd get up early tomorrow and read the reports then, he promised himself.

His last thought before he fell asleep that night was that Maya's nipples were pink. A pale, pretty pink!

Chapter 3

"I'm sorry but...you're...what?" Maya demanded, folding her arms over her chest as she glared at Sandoor. She'd gotten about four hours of sleep, so perhaps she'd misheard her friend...uh...fiancé's announcement.

"It's just for this weekend," Sandoor promised, reaching to pull her into his arms. But Maya stepped away, out of reach.

"Let me get this straight," she snapped, ignoring Sandoor's puppy-dog eyes. He pulled out that hound-dog expression whenever he knew he'd messed up, begging for forgiveness because he was so cute.

It wouldn't work this time! "You dragged me all the way out here just to introduce me to your brother. A brother that didn't even know that I was coming, I might add. Now you're leaving me here, in a strange country and with a man I barely know," she didn't mention that the last three nights she'd had sweet, private conversations with Jahlil over warm milk. "Just so that you can go mountain climbing with your friends?"

"I know that this isn't great timing. I get that, seriously, I do. But I promise that this will be my last adventure before I settle down and dig into the books so that I can get my degree. You are right, Maya. I need to accept more responsibility."

Her eyes narrowed. "You mean, responsibilities like not abandoning your new fiancée just so that you can go rock climbing with your friends and leaving her with your family?"

Sandoor laughed. "Ah, you know it's not that bad!" he told her, taking her hands and pulling her around so that he could nudge her ribs. "You love me. Admit it."

"Not today," she muttered, pulling out of his arms and moving out of arm's reach. "I'm going to pack my bags, Sandoor. You go ahead and

20

climb your mountain. I've got better things to do than to sit around and wait for you."

She heard his sigh, but remained strong and determined. "Ah, don't be mad, honey."

Maya shook her head in exasperation, but kept walking. "I'm not mad, Sandoor. I'm resigned. And I really do need to get back. I shouldn't even have come here. There was no need for me to meet your brother yet. We're not even officially engaged yet."

"We are!" he teased, rushing to her side and lifting her hand. "See? You're wearing my ring. And it looks so beautiful on you!"

She pulled her hand gently away. For some reason, Sandoor touching her lately didn't feel...right. Although, thinking of it now, they'd never even really kissed each other. Oh, Sandoor kissed her cheek or her fingers. Occasionally, he kissed the top of her head. But his affection felt... brotherly.

Had she missed something?

Or were her reservations that Sandoor wasn't the right man for her just her imagination? She'd always thought that his reserved affection was simply because she'd told him that she wasn't ready for an intimate relationship. But was there something else holding her back on becoming more intimate? Was there something deeper going on?

Unfortunately, that wasn't something she could answer while staying in this beautiful palace. Instinctively, she knew Jahlil was a distraction from figuring out her romantic issues with Sandoor. She needed space to think, to figure out whatever the issue was. "I have to go, Sandoor. You know I still need to pack up my apartment and get settled before I start my new job."

His dark, beautiful eyes were pleading. "Just a few more days, Maya! Please?" he begged, taking her hand and kissing her fingertips.

Maya resisted the urge to cringe and pull her hand away. This was right, she thought firmly. Sandoor was a sweet, gentle man. He was fun, witty, and he was exactly what she needed in her life. She was too serious, she reminded herself. She needed Sandoor in her life.

So, why did she dream about Jahlil every night? And why was it that Sandoor's touches felt...brotherly? Did he feel the same way?

"I promise, it will be better when we get back," he promised. "Mike just really wants this last trip."

Mike. Why did the sound of his name cause doubt to well up in her mind? She'd met Mike several times. He was a very nice guy!

"Is it just you and Mike this time?" she asked, heading towards the suite of rooms where she'd been staying, intending to pack up her bags and book a flight to Boston. She was going home. There was no reason to stay here, and she'd feel weird staying here without Sandoor.

"Nah!" Sandoor laughed. "Mike is bringing Greg and Charles too. The four of us are going to climb a cliff face this time."

That caught her attention. Maya stopped in the middle of the hallway, turning to stare up at Sandoor. "A cliff face?" she repeated, frowning up at Sandoor's sweet, guileless face. "That's not mountain climbing, Sandoor. That's more like...well, that's more like rock climbing. You need training to do something like that. Isn't it dangerous for a beginner?"

Sandoor grinned, excitement sparkling in his eyes. "Absolutely! But we'll be fine," he promised, putting a reassuring hand on her shoulder. "Don't worry about us. We'll be experts by the time we get to the top."

Maya pulled away as anger flooded through her. "Sandoor, you're not an expert! You've climbed a rock face about twenty feet up, exactly once. That does NOT make you an expert!"

He laughed, patting the back of her hand as if trying to soothe her. Maya jerked her hand away. "You're going to get hurt!" she retorted. But when the belligerent expression entered his eyes, Maya changed tactics. "Please, don't do this." She moved closer, putting a hand on his chest. "I have a terrible feeling about this trip."

Instantly, his features cleared of that annoying stubbornness and he laughed, pulling her in for a hug. "That bad feeling is just because you don't know my brother very well. But trust me. He's a great guy. Any time I have had a problem, he's been there for me." He kissed the top of her head. "Promise me that you'll stay until I get back? Then we can fly back to Boston together. I'll even help you pack up your place for the move."

She shook her head and pulled away, glaring up at him. "No, you won't. You'll order pizza, sit on my couch, and tell me what I'm doing wrong while *I* pack up."

He laughed, nodding his head. "Yeah, you're right. That's a much better plan and takes into account my lazy attitude towards any sort of physical exertion." He playfully nudged her arm. "Just don't start without me, okay?"

Maya sighed, rubbing her forehead. "I make no promises. You go do what you want to do, and I'll do my own thing."

He grabbed her, playfully lifting her in the air until she squealed, laughing as she demanded that he put her down. When he finally did, she leaned her head against his shoulder. "You're such a goofball," she told him.

He kissed her forehead. "Yeah. I know. But I'm *your* goofball."

Jahlil watched the two talk quietly together, their easy banter and laughing creating a strange ache in his chest. Jahlil wasn't jealous of his fun, loveable brother. He couldn't be. So, what was this unfamiliar emotion he was feeling?

With an irritated sigh, he headed for his next meeting. Sitting down, he nodded to the person briefing him on…? Hell, he had no idea what this meeting was about, nor did he care. Not today. His thoughts centered on Maya and the way she'd laughed when Sandoor picked her up. Jahlil had never been that casual with the women he'd taken to bed. Did he even want something like that?

No, he thought, looking at the papers in front of him. Jahlil knew that he wasn't a silly, playful sort. He wouldn't even know where to start.

Forcing his thoughts back to the present, he tried to concentrate on the meeting. But he didn't see the economic data. All he could see was Maya and her smiles, her gentle teasing late at night during their quiet conversations. And Sandoor kissing her.

Something occurred to him. He thought back to the way they had interacted. Sandoor was fun and affectionate, but he never kissed Maya. Not really. Not in a romantic sort of way.

Was Jahlil missing the point? Or was there something…odd in the way they interacted? He played out the scenes of them together over the past three days. No, Sandoor hadn't shown much passion at all in his interactions with Maya. So what was it that bothered him so much about them?

Chapter 4

Maya hummed as she folded a sweater, addng it to the stack of sweaters she'd already packed in her suitcase.

A fog of desolation that had overwhelmed her over the past couple of days. She hadn't heard from Sandoor yet, but he was supposed to come home today and...well, she kept thinking about Jahlil and how much she was going to miss their late night conversations.

He wasn't nearly as intimidating as...okay, that wasn't true. Jahlil *was* intimidating. And over the past few days, spending so much time alone with Jahlil, Maya knew one thing. She couldn't marry Sandoor. Not because there was a strange, niggling sensation in the back of her mind that something was wrong with their relationship.

No, because she knew she had feelings for Jahlil. Bad, forbidden feelings. Unsisterly feelings!

She would never act on those feelings, she vowed. Maya promised herself that she'd leave tomorrow and never talk about Jahlil again. She'd try to never even think of him again. She'd have to break off the engagement, return the ring, and beg Sandoor to remain friends, because it was the right thing to do. Sandoor was one of the best friends she'd ever had. He was fun, cute, and sweet.

But there was no passion. None at all! She hadn't realized what was missing from their relationship until she'd woken up this morning, remembering yet another passionate dream she'd had. A dream that had starred none other than the mighty and super-secretive, terrifyingly large and intimidating Jahlil. Yes, Maya admitted, silently to herself, she had very strong, very inappropriate feelings for her fiancé's brother. Feelings that were so forbidden, so wrong on so many levels, that she knew she had to do the honorable thing and break off her engagement with Sandoor as soon as possible.

But...should she wait until he'd finished his degree? Maybe she should talk to Jahlil and ask his opinion. She felt...a kinship. Was that the right word? Or maybe "connection" was a better term. Maya paused, trying to figure out what it was about Jahlil that made her feel as if she could talk to him about anything. And yet, when he looked at her, there was a strange sensation that she couldn't really describe. It wasn't a comfortable sensation. It was decidedly...uncomfortable! She really didn't like it.

"I'm a mess!" she muttered, laughing at herself. Picking up another sweater, she carefully folded and placed it in her suitcase. She'd be glad to head back home, get away from these conflicting emotions that were probably better left alone. Unexamined.

Sandoor was a good man, she reminded herself. A fun-loving, sweet, tender, and generous man. But he wasn't the man for her. That had become painfully obvious this week. Some woman...she paused, thinking about Mike and...now why did Mike's image pop up every time she thought of someone more compatible with Sandoor?

"Strange," she whispered. "Very strange."

A knock on the door startled her and she turned, staring at the closed door. For some reason, she felt that strange, uncomfortable tension build up within her. "You're being silly," she muttered, squaring her shoulders before walking over to the door. Pulling it open, she almost gasped when she saw Jahlil standing there. For a brief moment, she'd thought he'd come to see her...for a special reason.

Then she saw the look in his eyes.

"What's wrong?" she demanded, forgetting her fears and grabbing his hand, drawing him closer as if she could somehow ease whatever was hurting him so badly.

"We...need to talk," he said, his deep voice cracking slightly.

"Of course," she replied, stepping back and dropping his hand. "Please, come in."

Jahlil stepped into the suite and looked down at her, those dark eyes still filled with pain. He opened his mouth to say something, then stopped and sighed. "Let's sit down," he stalled. Again, Maya heard an odd note in his voice. It sent shivers of warning racing down her spine.

"Jahlil, what happened? What's wrong?" she asked as she trailed after him to the sitting room.

"Please," he said, gesturing to the sofa behind her, "sit down and..." he pressed his lips together, unable to continue.

Maya sat. Not because she needed to, but because Jahlil needed her to sit. And perhaps, Jahlil needed to sit too.

"Okay, I'm sitting. You're sitting. What's wrong? What happened?"

she urged.

He opened his mouth, then closed it again. Maya realized that he was clenching his hands so tightly his knuckles turned white. She reached out, covering his hands with one of her own.

In that moment, dread filled her. Suddenly, whatever it was that Jahlil had come to tell her…she didn't want to hear! She didn't want to know! Somehow, Maya needed to stop his next words from being spoken! Frantically, she considered putting a hand over his mouth, forcing him to stop before he said something that would devastate her.

"Sandoor…" he paused, closing his eyes for a moment as his fingers tightened around hers. "Sandoor was in an accident," he continued. The pain in his eyes was nearly blinding now. It was raw and brutal, relentless and uncompromising. "The group he was with started climbing a cliff face. Sandoor…" he paused, closing his eyes again as pain lashed across his face. He swallowed hard and Maya couldn't breathe. Jahlil opened his eyes and continued, "…didn't put his pin in the right place or…not deep enough," he paused, his head bowed.

"No!" Maya whispered, her hands itching, her fingers trembling as he spoke the words that she didn't want to hear. "Don't!"

"He fell…" Jahlil continued, then he stopped again, the pain obviously too much for him. "He fell and…"

"Stop!" she yelled, standing up and backing away from Jahlil. Maya wasn't aware of her tears. Her only conscious thought was to stop him from saying something that would shatter her world. Shaking her head, she continued to back up.

Jahlil's dark eyes lifted and Maya knew. She just knew! "He didn't survive, Maya," he explained, voice barely above a whisper.

"No!" she shrieked, holding her hands out in front of her. "No! I don't believe you!" Not Sandoor! He couldn't have fallen! He was fine! This was just a misunderstanding!

Maya shook her head, silently pleading with him to take it back. She crumpled slightly and barely managed to stay on her feet. "He takes stupid risks! He does stupid things but he's always fine! He has to be fine!"

Jahlil didn't move. Through the haze of her pain, she wondered what was going through his heart. Instinctively, she knew that Jahlil was hurting just as much as she was. No, that wasn't possible. She'd only known Sandoor for a couple of years. Jahlil had lost his baby brother. The brother that he'd loved more than anyone in the world!

"Oh Jahlil!" she whispered as compassion broke through her pain. She moved to his side and wrapped her arms around him. She felt him stiffen momentarily, but Maya tightened her hold, trying to take away some of his pain. He shuddered, and then his arms wrapped around her. She'd been sitting beside him on the couch, but before she could blink, she was on his lap, and she buried her face against his neck as she cried.

She sobbed with the pain of losing the most wonderful, amazing man she'd ever known. No, she hadn't loved him as a fiancée should. And that made her cry even harder, thinking of all of the times he'd begged her to marry him. She'd betrayed Sandoor! She hadn't loved him as deeply as she should have. And that was so wrong! She'd always sensed a pain underneath Sandoor's relentless laughter, but she'd never understood it. Never taken the time to understand what he really felt or thought or hoped for. Maya had asked occasionally, but Sandoor didn't enjoy serious conversations, so she'd just let it go.

Shame on her! And her shame multiplied the pain that overwhelmed her.

Jahlil held Maya for a long time. In an odd way, her tears and the soft warmth of her body pressed against his seemed to ease the ache of his own grief just a little. Oh, it was still there, still throbbing in his soul. But it was a little more bearable now. It was as if Maya's touch helped him deal with the almost unbearable loss of his brother.

He had no idea what she was feeling, but her sobs wracked her slender frame and he tightened his arms around her. She must have loved Sandoor more than he'd realized. Before Sandoor had left on his adventure, Jahlil had observed them together. They'd always appeared more like brother and sister than lovers. And he knew that Maya had never snuck into Sandoor's suite at night. They slept separately, they acted separately, only coming together for meals or adventures. How often had Jahlil found Maya in the library, reading quietly while Sandoor was out riding across the desert? Or in the kitchen, baking with the kitchen staff because, according to her words, baking comforted her.

He'd never heard such nonsense before, but then, what did he know about baking? He had too many meetings and issues to deal with to waste time in a kitchen. No matter how intriguing the thought might be, he knew that baking would never be on his agenda.

His arms tightened around Maya and he felt her snuggle closer. A sniff. Another sob, but she took a deep, steadying breath. He knew that he should let her go. Let her get back to her packing. But he couldn't. Right now, he needed her. He needed her in his arms to keep the pain at bay. It was almost as if Maya's touch was the only thing that was holding him together as he mentally sifted through the memories of his little brother.

How many times had he had to help Sandoor out of some mess or other? Too many to count, Jahlil thought. Maybe if Jahlil hadn't helped Sandoor so often over the years, maybe, he would still be alive!

No, that wasn't right, he reminded himself. Sandoor loved danger and adventure too much. He loved life and embraced it. If Jahlil had thought that there was something special between his brother and this guy, Mike, then that was just...well, perhaps it was wishful thinking. His arms tightened around Maya again and he resisted the urge to kiss the top of her head, to run his fingers through her hair or to touch her soft skin.

Yes, he could lose himself in Maya. He knew that he could find solace in her sweetness and her innocence. And yes, he knew that Maya was innocent. She might be intelligent and ambitious, but when it came to love and men, she was...!

"*His*" popped into his mind. But that was wrong! He'd thought that word several times over the past week and he'd stopped himself each time. Maya wasn't his woman. She was Sandoor's fiancée. And obviously, she'd loved him very deeply.

"Are you okay?" she whispered.

"I'm fine," he replied automatically.

Jahlil felt her shift slightly on his lap and he tightened his hold around her. Thankfully, she settled back against him and the weight of her, the softness of her body and her sweet breath against his neck soothed him. Her weight kept him grounded. Her softness kept the harsh world away. At least for a moment. He'd come back to the real world soon. Jahlil just needed a few more minutes of holding Maya in his arms.

Just a few more minutes.

He knew the exact moment she fell asleep. Her breathing slowed into a steady rhythm and Jahlil carefully shifted so that he was more comfortable. For a long time, it might have been minutes or hours, he held Maya in his arms, staring up at the ceiling as he thought about Sandoor. About his brother's love of life and the almost desperate way he tried to find laughter in the world.

Maya woke up with a start. It was dark now. When had the sun set? And why was she so warm? Looking down, she realized that she was lying on top of Jahlil. She was literally draped over him, her legs tangled with his.

She stared at his sleeping face for a long time. He was such a ruggedly handsome man. His thin nose and harsh cheekbones were so much like Sandoor's, and yet, they were also dramatically different. His tanned skin and the harsh lines of his face whispered of a very different life.

One of responsibility and someone who confronted the painful realities of life.

Sandoor never had to face reality, she thought. He ran from it. He hid from it. Jahlil...he'd never hide from anything. He'd face it head on. She smiled, picturing Jahlil in a bullfighter's ring. He was the defender of civilization while the bull was the pain of the real word, bashing at the doors to his country. But Jahlil wouldn't let the bad stuff in. He'd fight that bull and keep everyone safe.

Just as he'd done for her last night. He'd comforted her. Despite the overwhelming burdens of his everyday responsibilities, not to mention his own grief, Jahlil had shown her kindness. She doubted anyone had ever shown Jahlil kindness. He gave in the form of mercy and economic growth, ensuring a fair legal system for the people in his country. But who protected him? Who did he turn to when he was sad or weak or...she smiled slightly. She couldn't imagine Jahlil feeling weak. No, he was too strong. She doubted it was in his nature to feel weak.

She shifted, thinking to give the poor man a little breathing room. But as soon as she started to move, he opened his eyes and said, "Don't go," in a rough, pain filled voice.

Maya blinked at him, startled by his request. Because of that look, she stopped moving and settled back against him. He couldn't be comfortable. She was too heavy to be lying on top of him like this. But if it pushed that brutal pain in his eyes away, she'd stay here for as long as he needed her to.

It only took a couple moments before she fell asleep again. There was something about the gentle way that he held her, his hands on her back and shoulder, and the strong, steady rhythm of his heart pounding under her ear, that soothed her.

Chapter 5

The funeral was miserable! It was hot, of course. But it wasn't just the heat. It was…everything! Her hidden guilt was nearly overwhelming, because she knew she hadn't loved Sandoor the way she should have. That only added to the unbearable sadness of the event, and the mourning crowds that lined the streets, grieving the loss of their happy-go-lucky prince. This was a brutally somber event and there wasn't a dry eye to be seen.

Except Jahlil. He walked stoically behind the carriage carrying Sandoor's casket, his features carefully blank. Maya walked beside him, her face hidden behind dark sunglasses and shielded with a large, brimmed hat.

Maya felt wrong about being in the family procession. She wasn't a member of this family. She hadn't gotten to the wedding and, worse, Maya knew, deep down, that she never would have. She should have told Sandoor she didn't love him as a wife should. She should tell Jahlil that she hadn't been a loving fiancée to his brother. But Jahlil had insisted. He'd explained that she *was* a member of the family, if only because she wore Sandoor's engagement ring.

Maya would have argued, but she saw the pain and determination in Jahlil's eyes and knew that he needed her. It wasn't because she was a member of the family. It was because…because he needed her. And that gave her the strength to continue along the street to the family crypt where Sandoor's body would be interred.

This procession wasn't just for her and Jahlil. The funeral, ceremony, and procession, were for the citizens of Celina. They needed one last goodbye for their adventurous, fun-loving prince. Sandoor might have been irresponsible regarding his responsibilities, but the citizens of Celina adored him. They admired his whole-hearted embrace of life, love, and happiness.

What's more, they respected Jahlil. He was their leader and they loved him even more. Every few minutes, someone standing on the streets would break the somber silence and call out to Jahlil, offering words of condolences. Sometimes, they called out to her as well. But Maya simply bowed her head, stifling the tears that kept coming at the most inopportune moments. Thankfully, for the most part, she got through the ordeal with just trembling lips and a determination to not shame Jahlil. She had to be here to support him. She might not have loved Sandoor as a wife, but she'd love him as a close, beloved friend.

With that in mind, she lifted her head higher, determined to emulate Jahlil. She could be strong. At least, she could be outwardly strong! Jahlil had helped her through this ordeal, so she'd do whatever she had to in order to help him.

But when the time came for the casket to be interred, Maya couldn't watch. She couldn't stand by and see her wonderful friend be pushed into a cold, unfeeling block of marble.

Instead, she looked around at the others standing near the crypt. It was a beautiful, sunny day. Not too hot, thankfully. That's when her eyes landed on Mike. Sandoor's friend looked as if he'd gone through hell. His hair was rumpled, his tie was askew, and his eyes were red from crying. The pain in his eyes was almost tangible! Once again, Maya wondered if there was more to Sandoor's friendship with Mike.

She turned her attention back to Jahlil. He was painfully still. The minister spoke a few words. And damn it, she hated the restrictions on public displays. Forget all of that! She reached out and took Jahlil's hand! For a moment, he didn't respond and she felt silly. But then his fingers squeezed hers. She tightened her grip, feeling the pain inside of him.

Maya wanted to lean against him, to silently offer him strength. But she kept herself very still, knowing that Jahlil had to appear strong, even during this most horrible moment. Nothing in his world was private, she thought sadly.

Except for that night when he'd held her in his arms. They'd shared something that night. She'd felt a connection to Jahlil from the moment she'd met him, but that night...the connection between the two of them had grown and strengthened. Maya didn't fully understand how their relationship had changed. But it had. It frightened her in some ways, and comforted her in others.

Jahlil walked into his office, feeling a sense of...grim finality. Sandoor was gone. His funeral was over. He had a mountain of work that he needed to sift through. But instead, he turned his back on his responsibilities.

Maya needed...? He stopped himself from assuming that she needed him. She wasn't his woman, he reminded himself for the millionth time. Still, he thought of something that might help her through the next few days and weeks. At least, he hoped it would.

There was a bit of startled chaos when he stepped into the stables. Normally, his assistant would have called ahead to warn the stable hands that he was on his way. They would have had his horse saddled and standing ready for him.

But he wasn't here to ride.

"My apologies, Your Highness!" the stable manager exclaimed, bowing as he rushed forward. "We were not informed of your imminent arrival. I'll have your horse readied personally!"

"That's not necessary," Jahlil replied, holding up a hand to stop the man's eager efforts. "I'm not here for a ride."

The man bowed again. "Of course." He looked around worriedly. "How can I assist you?'

Jahlil felt ridiculous. But he knew his idea would soothe Maya. "The kittens," he said, rubbing the back of his neck awkwardly. "I saw them several weeks ago, just after their birth. Are they weaned yet? Or do they still need their mother?"

The stable manager blinked in surprise.

"The...kittens, Your Highness?"

Jahlil wanted to laugh at the man's obvious confusion. "Yes. The kittens. Are they weaned? I was...I wanted to give one a new home."

The stable manager shook his head. "I will happily take care of that, Your Highness. We give them to–"

Jahlil lifted his hand in the air, gently silencing the man. "I need one," Jahlil interrupted firmly.

The man stared for another moment in stunned surprise, but he rallied quickly. "Of course! This way!" and he led Jahlil into one of the stalls where the small kittens were scampering about. They were still tiny little fluff balls, but they no longer needed their mother. In fact, the momma cat was already gone, out hunting or whatever it was cats did during the day.

Jahlil bent down, examining each kitten. There were five in all and he had to admit that they were all pretty adorable. But which would be best? This was such an important decision. He almost laughed at how seriously he was taking this decision. He could snap off orders with military precision. But the selection of a kitten clearly required more effort.

One toddled over to him, staring up at Jahlil with huge golden eyes. The kitten meowed demandingly, then jumped onto his bent knee, balancing by digging its tiny claws into his slacks.

"I'm so sorry, Your Highness," the stable manager gasped, rushing forward to take the kitten away, as if the tiny creature had done something heinous instead of simply doing what kittens do.

"Its fine," Jahlil replied, chuckling as he stood up, the tiny creature cradled in his arms. "This one is perfect," he told the man. Then turned and walked back into the palace.

At the abrupt knock, Maya opened the door, feeling a sharp stab of pain when she spotted Jahlil standing in her doorway.

"Hi," she whispered, leaning her forehead against the door.

"Hi," he replied in his usual commanding voice. "May I come in? I have something for you."

Maya's mouth fell open. "Jahlil, I don't need..." She stopped when he revealed the tiny ball of fluff he'd been hiding behind his back. "Oh!" she gasped, moving forward to accept the tiny kitten. "You are so adorable!" And then she laughed.

Laughed! She'd actually laughed! After the past week, a week filled with sobbing, grief, formal funeral events and...seemingly endless visits from the various dignitaries from all over the world...Maya hadn't thought she'd never laugh again.

The tiny creature mewed, batting at a lock of her hair. "Where did you come from?" she asked the tiny creature.

"He...or she," Jahlil sighed, rubbing the back of his neck, looking as if he felt completely out of place. "I didn't take the time to check its gender, to be honest. I was looking for other aspects."

She turned and looked up at him, once again startled by how handsome and amazingly wonderful Jahlil was. At this particular moment, she thought he looked even more handsome than ever. Behind all that royal harshness and male arrogance, there was a touching hint of awkwardness. It was almost as if he were embarrassed to give her the kitten.

"What aspects do you look for in a kitten?" she asked, charmed and intrigued as she brought the adorable creature to her cheek. Immediately, the kitten started purring like a jet engine! For such a tiny thing, its purr was loud!

Jahlil shifted uncomfortably on his feet, looking at something behind her. "Cuteness," he mumbled.

Maya was so stunned, she couldn't react for a long moment. Then she cracked up, her eyes sparkling. "You were looking for cuteness?"

Jahlil sighed and shuffled his feet again. She watched with amusement as he rubbed the back of his neck. "I picked this one out for you. I know that you're leaving us today, although I still think you should stay and live in the palace."

Maya's eyes softened. They'd had this conversation several times already and she sincerely appreciated his offer. "You know I can't do that, Jahlil," she said, smiling as she cuddled the kitten closer. "I have to go home. I have to get back to my life."

"You could have a life here," he pointed out, pacing back and forth. "I could create a job for you here."

She laughed again, tamping down on the swelling of the unnamed emotion that welled up in her throat whenever Jahlil was present. Or not present. It was that same emotion that she refused to define, and refused to examine too carefully. It was an emotion that felt like a betrayal of Sandoor.

"I appreciate the charity, but I need to make it on my own," she told him.

"What are you going to do?" he asked, furious all over again on her behalf when he remembered how she'd lost the job in Boston because the company had filled her position with someone else when she hadn't arrived on the start date. "I can still call that company," he offered. "I have enough power to get your job back. You stayed here for Sandoor. You shouldn't be penalized for the generous gift of your time."

Maya lowered her eyes, not bothering to tell him that she hadn't stayed out of respect for Sandoor. She'd grieved for her lost friend. She'd always miss him. Sandoor had been a wonderful person and one of her best friends. But he hadn't been the love of her life. She'd known that almost immediately upon arriving here.

Almost immediately upon meeting Jahlil.

Okay, that was one of those forbidden thoughts that she didn't want to have!

The only thing she'd allow herself to admit was that she'd stayed here in Celina, not for Sandoor, but for Jahlil. He'd never admit it, but he'd needed her. He'd needed her in ways that...again, she wasn't going to define. Together, they'd gotten through the past month. Day by day, they'd talked about Sandoor. Over dinner, she'd told him about how she'd met Sandoor, the way he'd teased her into leaving her studies to have a picnic. On another morning, Jahlil told her about how Sandoor had climbed too high into a tree one day. Jahlil had climbed up to help his little brother down, showing him step by step how to get out of the tree. She'd laughed at the story, awed by Jahlil's bravery as well as his obvious love for his little brother. No matter how many times Sandoor got into trouble, Jahlil rescued him.

And Maya lov…greatly respected Jahlil.

Coming back to the present, she turned and smiled up at Jahlil. "I know that you have the power to fix just about anything," she teased. "But my career isn't something that I need you to fix, Jahlil. I have to do this on my own. I've gotten my degree, and now I need to go out into the world and prove to myself that I'm good enough."

She saw the muscle flex in his jaw and knew that he didn't agree with her. He was a lion. A protective lion, who was willing to take her into his household and protect her, even though she wasn't even a member of his family. "What are you going to do?"

She shrugged. "I don't know. I know that you paid the rent on my apartment for the next year," she stated, watching his features. There was no embarrassment at his generosity being discovered. Just a slight lifting of one of those dark eyebrows, as if challenging her to remonstrate him for that generosity. "And I have some ideas on what I'd like to do."

"Care to share?" he asked, an almost teasing note to his voice. But Jahlil never teased. Did he?

"No," she laughed, untangling a kitten claw from her shirt. "If I tell you what I'm planning, then you'll step in and interfere." She looked up at him. "In a kind and generous way of course. But I'm not going to let you do that. You've done more than enough already."

As she cuddled the kitten, the sparkle on her hand reminded her of one last thing she needed to do. Slipping the enormous ring off, she held it out to Jahlil. "Here," she said. "This isn't mine anymore."

"Keep it," he retorted, folding his arms over his massive chest as that arrogance came washing back into his demeanor. "Sandoor gave it to you. It's yours."

She shook her head. "No, it's too expensive. And I never married Sandoor. It's *not* mine."

"It's yours, Maya," he replied firmly.

She smiled up at him. "I'm not taking it, Jahlil," she said, moving over to the coffee table and setting the huge ring down. "Thank you for the kitten. I'll bring him back to the stables."

"The kitten is yours, if you want it." His gaze sharpened slightly as he watched the scrap of fluff sitting on her shoulder, batting at Maya's earring. He sighed. "And you're flying home on my private plane. My assistant has already cleared the way for you to bring the animal into the United States, so you won't have to deal with customs."

She smiled up at him. "I can keep it?" she asked, awed by the wonderful gift. "Seriously?"

He chuckled and the sound sent that now-predictable shiver racing down her spine.

"Seriously, Maya. The kitten is yours if it will help you feel better," he replied. His gaze turned serious. "You *will* call me if you have any problems, won't you?" he commanded. It wasn't really a question. "You're under my protection now."

She smiled, and did something daring. Moving forward, she snuggled her new kitten against her side as she hugged Jahlil. "I promise, I will call you if anything happens."

He hugged her back, and Maya smiled at the awkwardness of his gesture. This man was not hugged enough, she thought.

Stepping back before she did something foolish, like kiss him...she smiled up at him. "Thank you for the kitten," she said.

He looked around, that awkwardness right back in place. "Well, right." He sighed. "Take the ring. And the kitten. Sell the ring."

She laughed. "I'll take the kitten," she told him.

Jahlil growled as he turned and left her suite.

Chapter 6

Five Years Later...

"Uh...Sire?" Ormond interrupted.

Jahlil glanced up from the report on troop morale that he was reading and glared at his assistant. He wasn't irritated that his assistant had interrupted his concentration so much as he was irritated that he had to even read this stuff. Seriously? Couldn't his generals take care of this stuff and summarize it for him? Why the hell had they sent him a ten page document?

He cared very deeply about the morale in his military. It was essential to have good morale, otherwise, the soldiers wouldn't fight as hard, wouldn't care about their mission. But seriously, a ten page report? Couldn't his generals give him a thumbs up or down, with a list of changes they want to incorporate into the training regimens?

But Ormond looked wary and, speaking of morale, Jahlil dug deep for a little more patience and cleared his expression of annoyance. "What's on your mind?" he finally asked of his normally intrepid assistant.

The man stepped into Jahlil's office, but continued to hover near the door. Whatever Ormond had to say was bad news. Jahlil braced himself for more long, sleepless nights. Not that he'd had many deep, wonderful full nights of sleep lately.

Jahlil glanced at the calendar on his computer, wincing when he realized that it had been a month since he'd seen her last. The trees in the Northeast had just started to change color back then as the fall weather creeped in. Thinking of that, he thought about Maya's beautiful smile as she'd admired the glorious colors on the trees. The Boston area truly was astonishingly beautiful in the fall. The leaves changed from green to brilliant shades of orange, yellow, red, and even purple.

And fall was Maya's favorite season. Unfortunately, the following

38

months of winter weren't as beautiful. Maya hated Boston winters. They were long and miserable, frigid and snowy. There were plenty of places around the world that received a great deal of snow, so he didn't assume that Boston had a priority on the miserable stuff. But Maya truly hated the shorter days that were overcast much of the time. He suspected that she suffered from a mild case of seasonal affective disorder, but he hadn't yet figured out how to help her.

Other than having her come live in Celina. She'd have sunshine all year round, he thought. Yes, that could be the ideal solution.

But...Maya still wasn't his woman. She was his responsibility though, and that was why he worried about her so often.

Jahlil almost laughed at that last thought. Hell, he didn't think about Maya because she was his responsibility. And yet, she hadn't truly been his responsibility for five, long, tedious years. He'd love for her to be his responsibility. He'd love to have the right to care for her and tease her into smiling. He'd love to ensure that she ate enough and slept enough...he'd love to take care of her.

He loved her. He'd accepted this fact about a year after she'd returned home after Sandoor's funeral. He loved her more deeply than he'd ever thought possible. And it had nothing to do with her previous engagement to his younger brother.

In fact, he couldn't ask her out on an official date *because* she'd been engaged to his younger brother. Damn Sandoor for dying! Damn him for leaving Maya all alone in this world! She'd loved Sandoor so deeply. He noticed her affection for his brother every time they talked during their sporadic dinners together. During every meal, they shared stories about Sandoor and she'd tell him what the two of them had planned for their future together.

In other words, Maya obviously still hadn't gotten over Sandoor. Damn him!

"Your Highness?" Ormond prompted.

Jahlil's thoughts snapped back to the present. His assistant was in front of his desk. Apparently, the shorter man had already explained the whole situation while Jahlil had been thinking about Maya.

"I'm sorry, Ormond," Jahlil apologized with a heavy sigh. He lifted the report in his hand, pretending as if it had distracted him. Better for Ormond to assume that Jahlil had been thinking about troop morale instead of the reality; that he'd been thinking about Maya. Again.

"I apologize," Ormond said, bowing slightly. "I interrupted your reading," and he bowed. "This was the wrong time to bring this to you."

Suppressing another burst of annoyance, Jahlil tossed the report onto his desk. "Please, Ormond," he said, waving the man forward. "You know my schedule extremely well, so if you felt it necessary to interrupt me, then it must be important. I apologize for not giving you my full attention." He leaned back in his leather chair, lacing his fingers over his stomach before nodding to Ormond. "Go ahead. You have my full attention now."

Ormond clasped his fingers together. "We've received word from the Ambassador of Brumadi, Your Highness," he said softly, looking as if he'd like to back away.

Jahlil's attention sharpened. "What's that bastard done now?" he demanded. He took a deep breath, hoping he was prepared for whatever horrific news was about to be shared.

"Actually, it's not the normal ambassador, Your Highness. This person...well, surprisingly this message came from back door sources."

That *was* surprising. Brumadi was one of his country's most hated enemies. For decades, there had been skirmishes off the coast of Celina with the Brumadi Navy or in the air space. He wasn't sure if he hated the Brumadi government, or his enemy to the south, Dilaar and the despised Sheik el Moussa more. So, if someone from Brumadi had ventured into enemy territory, and through back channel maneuvering instead of the more abrasive Brumadi embassy, Jahlil was intrigued. "What's going on?"

"A summit," Ormond whispered, as if the idea was too outrageous to contemplate. "A peace treaty."

Jahlil was too stunned to speak for a long moment. It took him a moment to make sense of the conversation. "Between Celina and Brumadi?" he asked, his eyebrows rising. "Why? Is el Hasan," he said, referencing the Sheik of Brumadi, "trying to get me to gang up against Dilaar?" he asked. "Because there's no way we could–"

"No," Ormond interrupted, shaking his head. The man scanned the room as if expecting someone to jump out of the shadows. Was Ormond expecting someone else to be in Jahlil's office? "All three leaders!" Ormond hissed. "In a secret place for a series of round table meetings to discuss a peace treaty."

Jahlil stared at the man, stunned. But, in a moment, he started to calculate the list of issues that would need to be resolved before three very different, powerful countries could come to some sort of peace treaty. There were many obstacles. However, if they could do it...!

Jahlil stood up, his fists braced on his desk. "All three of us? In the same room?"

Ormond nodded helplessly.

"That would be...!" He didn't say anything more. It was too wild of an idea. He stared down at the papers on his desk. A peace treaty. What would that entail? How could they accomplish such a monumental feat? There would be so many moving parts, so many underlying issues between the three countries.

But if they could do it, if they could just start heading in that direction…! The money they all could save on defense! And the lives that would be saved! Hell, a peace treaty between the three countries could be…revolutionary!

Looking up, he realized that Ormond was waiting for a response. "When does he need an answer?"

The man shrugged. "A timeline has not yet been established."

Jahlil stood up, folding his arms as he stared thoughtfully out the window, not really seeing the magnificent mountains in the distance or his beautiful capital city laid out below. He was thinking about Maya. He wondered what she might think of a peace treaty.

Turning, he nodded firmly. "Yes!" he snapped. "Tell Monfuso," he said, referring to his own Ambassador to Brumadi, "to feel out the others. If the other two, or even just one of them are willing, then consider us in. But there would have to be precautions." His mind started whirling. A moment later, he started listing those precautions and Ormond noted them all down in his ever-ready tablet. For the next two hours, he went through the issues, playing out various arguments in his head. Yes, this was a wonderful thing, he thought. It was about time that they worked out their differences. It wasn't as if the three countries had been enemies for generations. The hostilities between the three of them had been brewing only for the past twenty years or so. That meant that opinions ran deep, but were not yet set in stone in the hearts and minds of his citizens.

This *could* happen. Under the right circumstances, this could actually work! As he considered the logistics, he remembered a place…a tiny island near…where was that island? In the Caribbean somewhere. But what was the name of that island?

When it came to him, he snapped his fingers, startling Ormond. "There's an island off of the coast of Belize. It's small, but beautiful. There's a resort there that will be safe enough. Suggest that for the face to face conversations."

Ormond nodded, typing frantically even as he headed for the doorway. "Yes, Your Highness," he replied absently.

"And contact Maya," Jahlil added, startling the man into turning around.

"Ms. Tisdale? You want to speak with her?" he asked, trying to understand.

Jahlil thought for a moment, wondering if his plan made sense. But as he considered options, he knew that this was the right thing to do. With a sharp nod, he confirmed his order. "Have her pack a bag for a tropical island. If she can get away from her job, I want her with us for the negotiations."

Ormond blinked, his fingers hovering above the virtual keyboard on his tablet. "You want her to participate in the negotiations, Sire?"

Jahlil laughed and shook his head. "Not a chance!" he replied. "I don't want her near those bastards." He thought about it for another moment. Was he making a mistake? He tossed the pros and cons around for a moment. No, this was the right thing to do. Nodding as if mentally confirming his thoughts, he glanced at his assistant. "Yes, Maya needs more sunshine during the winter months. See if she would be willing to come along. She won't participate in the discussions, but she can stay with me and relax for a week. Longer if she likes. It will help her if she gets some sunshine during the winter months. That should help her sleep patterns, as well as her moods during the grey days facing her in Boston."

"Yes, Your Highness," Ormond replied, understanding the tact dismissal. He started towards the door again, and bowed at the exit. Jahlil watched the older man leave. He suspected that his assistant didn't entirely approve of Maya. He wondered why, but wasn't in the mood to worry about it.

Besides, he loved the idea of spending a whole week with Maya. Jahlil had managed to spend some time with her over the years. Mostly, he was only able to carve out a dinner every couple of months. But a whole week! Yes, that would be...hellish. And heaven!

Was the idea of spending a week with Maya a bad idea?

This would be his last contact with her, he promised. He needed to move on. He needed to find a wife, produce an heir.

Immediately, the image of Maya popped into his mind. Maya lushly pregnant. Maya nursing their newborn. She had lovely breasts, he thought. His body hardened painfully and he bent over, fisting his hands on his desk again as he closed his eyes, forcing the woman from his thoughts.

Maya still loved Sandoor, he told himself. She was off-limits!

Chapter 7

Maya smiled as she read the message. "Typical Jahlil," she muttered, leaning back in her leather chair. Obviously, this was an invitation for Thumper to jump onto her lap. The tiny kitten Jahlil had given her had grown into an enormous, twenty pound cat! "Oh, so you think it's time for attention?" she teased, but automatically, she scratched Thumper's ears. "He wants me to talk to him," she told the massive cat. "In the Caribbean!"

Thumper wasn't overly impressed. He nudged her hand off the keyboard. "Hey!" she laughed, but continued petting him. His heavy purring always soothed her. As an added benefit, the sweetly ferocious cat continuously reminded her of Jahlil. Thumper was big and fierce when he wanted attention, then turned sweet and cuddly.

Okay, so Thumper wasn't particularly ferocious, but he always got his way. Just like Jahlil.

She turned back to the e-mail, reading through the details. *"A driver will pick you up and take you to the airport. A plane at Logan airport will be standing by to fly you here."*

She smiled, thinking of the big guy. "At least he's not flying into Boston to take me out to dinner again," she muttered to Thumper. "But I'm not sure if I want to spend a whole week with him on a warm, Caribbean island."

Thumper wasn't impressed with her dilemma.

For several moments, she contemplated her answer. She didn't want to see Jahlil again. Every time he flew into town, it took her several weeks, sometimes months, to stop thinking about him. He was so amazingly virile and male and...she loved him. Their dinner conversations were lively and challenging. He always took her to the best restaurants in town and he always had a beautiful, expensive dress hand-delivered to her door prior to their dinner "dates".

She looked down at Thumper who had his eyes closed, blissfully purring while Maya scratched behind his ears. "The dresses have become a bit sexier over the past year, haven't they?" she asked of her feline beast. His answer was a blinking of his golden eyes.

"I know! You don't approve either." She continued to scratch. "But I gotta tell you, my friend, every time I wear one of his dresses, I feel... amazing!"

She leaned back again, biting her lower lip as she contemplated the invitation. A whole week. In the tropics. With Jahlil!

"No," she said out loud, this time, more to herself than to the cat. "I can't do it. I just...I need to stop seeing him." Maya knew that her heart was so completely in love with Jahlil that it was time to stop seeing him. "Cold turkey," she told the cat. His ears twitched and his head swiveled in her direction, then he turned toward the kitchen where his food bowl was. A bowl that was probably empty. "Not you," she whispered, soothing her hungry beast. "Me. I have to stop seeing him. This obsession isn't healthy. I have to..." she swallowed past the lump in her throat, "get over Jahlil. I need to find someone else. Someone..." she stopped. The word "boring" popped into her mind.

"No!" she gasped, surprising Thumper into turning to glare at her. "I'm not going to find someone boring!" she vowed. "But I need to do something. I need to change my life." She looked down at Thumper who blinked up at her indignantly. "I'm not going to become a hermit who only talks to my cat!"

Turning back to her computer, she typed out her reply. "*We need to talk*," she started off. "*What time will the car pick me up?*" She could have easily gotten to the airport on her own. And Maya knew that there were daily flights to the island. So, she didn't *need* to have a personal chauffer pick her up and take her to the airport, and she definitely didn't need the private plane to fly her to the island. But she also knew that Jahlil wouldn't allow her to get there on her own. He was a bit stuffy about her personal safety.

Maya didn't allow herself to smile at that. She was a strong woman and didn't need a man to take care of her.

Even if she was madly in love with him.

Sighing, she turned back to work, refusing to check her e-mail for a response.

Chapter 8

The sun felt like a soothing blanket, warming her after the almost frigid air on the plane and the icy temperatures she'd left behind in Boston. Lifting her face up to the sunshine, she stood on the tarmac for a long moment, just letting the warmth and gentle humidity seep into her winter-dry skin.

"You look like a sun goddess," a deep voice called out.

Startled, Maya turned to find Jahlil coming towards her, his eyes hidden behind dark sunglasses. But she'd recognize him anywhere. He had only grown more muscular over the past few years. He was still shockingly attractive in that raw, powerful way. And every time she saw him, it was a shock to her system.

Shaking herself out of her momentary stupor, she smiled up at him. "We need to talk, Jahlil," she told him.

He smiled slightly, putting a hand to the small of her back. "I figured that was the case. Let's talk in private though."

"You're going to be difficult, aren't you?" she laughed up at him.

"Of course!" he replied cheerfully as he opened the door to the Jeep and gestured her inside. "Get in. I'm driving."

Her mouth fell open. "*You* are driving? Has hell frozen over?" she teased.

"Get in, brat," he growled.

She laughed as she climbed into the Jeep, settling into the comfortable seat. She watched hungrily as he came around to the driver's side, admiring the powerful way he moved. He always moved with absolute confidence, she thought. It was such an amazing thing to watch Jahlil.

With a sigh, she pushed her sunglasses higher, then waited while he climbed into the Jeep, refusing to watch him as he settled his tall, muscular frame next to her. Keep it cool, she silently told herself.

It was only a twenty minute drive to the resort, which was a beautiful yellow building surrounded by twenty additional buildings encircling a stunning courtyard filled with lush tropical plants, flowers bursting with color, and a small waterfall. She'd like to say that it was a charming place, but it was too big and too elegant to qualify as charming. But there was definitely a charming element to the site.

"This is lovely."

"Is this the only luggage you brought?" he asked, watching as one of the bell hops pulled a small suitcase out of the back of the Jeep.

"Yes. I didn't think I'd need much," she told him.

She almost laughed as his lips compressed in disapproval. "You think so, huh?" he asked, putting a hand to the small of her back.

"Well, we need to–"

"When we're alone," he repeated, but this time, he lowered his head so that his lips were very close to her ear. Maya couldn't stop the shiver of awareness when he did that, and she prayed that he didn't notice. The last thing she needed was for Jahlil to realize that she had personal feelings for him! Goodness, she couldn't repay his kindness over the years with an awkward moment when he realized she had a painful crush for him!

Okay, so it was a whole lot more than just a crush, she thought as she followed him through the beautiful lobby and into what she suspected was a private elevator.

Once inside the elevator cab, she stood awkwardly on one side while he stood in the middle and the bellhop remained on the other side. The poor man could obviously feel the tension, if his odd looks and darting eyes was any indication.

She breathed a sigh of relief when the elevator doors opened. The bellhop stepped out first, and he immediately moved off to deliver her suitcase into what she suspected was one of the guest bedrooms. Meanwhile, Maya looked around, taking in the glorious beauty of the space. "Wow! These windows looking out to the ocean must be pretty amazing to wake up to every morning."

He chuckled. "I don't get to see much of the view. I'm here for meetings."

"Ah, ever the serious leader." she teased.

He rolled his eyes. "Now that we're alone," he started, only to pause when the bellhop emerged from the bedroom. The poor guy looked at them, then literally stumbled out of the room, pulling the suite's doors closed behind him without waiting for a tip.

Jahlil turned to look at her again. "As I said," he paused, looking around and Maya laughed, "now that we're alone, what did you need to talk to me about?"

He walked over to what appeared to be a fully stocked bar, pulling out a bottle of white wine from a small refrigerator. With expertise, he uncorked the bottle and poured two glasses.

She watched, as always fascinated by his hands. Jahlil had long, tanned fingers and she remembered him holding Thumper so carefully as a kitten.

"Maya?" he prompted.

She blinked and realized that he was holding the glass of wine out to her.

"Oh! Sorry!" she gasped, taking the glass, careful not to touch his fingers. She might drop the glass if she had any contact with him. She knew from experience that touching Jahlil, even in the most casual way, would prompt a response in her body that was...well, embarrassing.

"Thank you," she whispered, taking a quick sip of her wine to camouflage the fact that her hands were shaking.

"You're welcome," he replied, then sat down across from her. "So, what's on your mind?"

It was the perfect opening, but still, she hesitated. She didn't want to hurt his feelings. She lov...respected him a great deal. He'd been so good to her over the years. But she knew that she needed to be firm.

"I need you to stop," she explained with as gentle a tone as she could manage.

He lifted a dark eyebrow quizzically as he peered at her over the rim of his wine glass. "Stop?"

"Yes," she replied. "Stop intimidating the men I go out with. Stop taking my car in the middle of the night and getting everything checked and the tires replaced. Stop with the food and meal deliveries when you think I'm not eating." She took a deep breath. "I know that you think that I'm your responsibility, Jahlil, but I need to move on with my life." Her voice cracked a little. She didn't want to move on. She wanted to throw herself into his arms and beg him to think of her as someone other than his little sister. She wanted to be his lover! She wanted to feel the heat of him against her skin and taste his kisses the way she'd done so often in her dreams.

But that was not to be, she reminded herself firmly, tightening her grip on the wine glass.

"You don't eat well," he pointed out calmly. "In fact, there are days when you don't leave your apartment and you forget to eat at all."

She lowered her head. "That's another thing. How do you know that I forget to eat?" she asked. "That's a bit creepy, Jahlil."

He laughed softly. "I don't know the specific days that you forget to eat, Maya," he replied calmly. "I just know that you go shopping on Thursday evenings. Except on the days when you forget. You purchase seven containers of yogurt, seven bananas, one loaf of bread, lunch meat, cheese, seven apples and a few other items that vary from week to week."

She stared at him, her mouth falling open. "How do you know that?" she demanded.

"Because I've assigned a body guard to watch over you," he explained. "You are *family*, Maya. It is my responsibility to take care of you."

She set the glass of wine down on the coffee table, then stood up and walked over to the window. "I don't want to be your responsibility, Jahlil. You have too many people who claim your time." She spun around, imploring him with her eyes to understand. "I've always wanted to be your...friend," she replied, hoping that he hadn't noticed her hesitation. "And if you're constantly checking up on me, then I'm only one more thing that you have to make sure is working properly."

He stood up as well, walking over to her. "And you want to be free of me?" he asked, his voice velvety smooth.

No! The word echoed in her mind immediately. But she swallowed the retort, forcing herself to nod instead. "Yes. It's time. You helped me through that period after Sandoor passed away," she told him, closing her eyes as she remembered the way he'd held her, the tender way he'd wiped her tears. She'd loved every moment of being in his arms and this "brotherly" affection was killing her. Slowly, it was wearing away every ounce of her will to see other men, to find that elusive happiness that she so desperately wanted to find with him, but knew deep in her heart that she couldn't. She had to move on!

He looked at her steadily and it took every ounce of self-discipline within her to keep from fidgeting.

"I'll make a deal with you," he offered.

Relieved, she released the breath she'd been holding. "What's that?"

"You stay here with me this week and relax. Get some sun because you're looking a little pale. And eat enough to gain a few pounds back. At the end of this week, then we'll discuss how to move forward."

She contemplated that for a long moment. Looking around, she accepted that there were worst fates she could face rather than spending a week in a luxurious vacation spot.

"And after this week, you'll let me fail if I fail?" she prompted.

He smiled, but his expression turned mysterious. "Let's just take it one day at a time."

Despite herself, she smiled at him. "That's a non-answer, Jahlil."

He chuckled and shrugged. "And that's the best I can give you right

now." He glanced at his watch and sighed. "Unfortunately, I have another meeting that I must attend."

She turned as well, confused as he moved towards the doorway. "Wait,
you want me to relax and have a good time, but you're going off to
some tedious meeting where you'll probably spend hours debating the
price of...corn and soybean or oil and natural gas? That doesn't seem
fair!"

He waved to her without responding, then vanished out the door.

Left alone, Maya wondered what she was supposed to do now. Looking around, she blinked at the beautiful suite. The beautiful, empty
suite! She was in a beautiful, romantic vacation spot. Alone. What fun
was that?

She walked through the suite, which was more like a penthouse with
five bedrooms, a full dining room, massive living room with floor to
ceiling windows looking out over the turquoise ocean, a surprisingly
large kitchen, a game room, music room complete with a grand piano,
as well as a movie room with a massive television that was larger than
the biggest wall in her apartment.

"Good grief," she muttered, walking back into the bedroom where
she'd found her suitcase. She unzipped it and pulled out the pretty sundress she'd packed. Just one sundress and her toiletries. She'd intended
to stay here just one night. "I guess I'd better hit the shops," she muttered.

For the next several hours, she shopped, buying a black bathing
suit, a red one, cover ups for both, a pair of sandals, and two pairs of
shorts with matching tops. And because she was here with Jahlil, she
also found two cocktail dresses, assuming that he'd take her out to a
nice restaurant at some point, as he normally did. He usually chose
the more upscale venues, but she smiled at the memory of when he'd
swooped into town to take her out to dinner, but she'd convinced him
to let her choose the restaurant. She'd taken him to the public gardens
that usually had the best food trucks. She'd ordered him to sit down
on a park bench, then Maya had disappeared to get their dinner. She'd
glanced back at him, understanding that he was painfully uncomfortable. But the meal she'd gotten from the food trucks had more than
made up for the less than stellar service and atmosphere.

"I can get those for you, ma'am," one of the bellhops said as soon as
she stepped out of the taxi that had brought her back to the resort.

"Oh!" she gasped, pulling back on her numerous bags. "No, that's okay.
I've got it."

The man looked horrified at the idea of her carrying her own bags.
And in the past, Maya knew that Jahlil demanded extraordinary service

from his staff and the places where he stayed.

But now that she was going to do this whole "vacationing" thing on her own, Maya needed to do this without the staff. No time like the present to begin!

As soon as she stepped into the suite, she knew that she was in trouble. Jahlil's bodyguards filled the suite, some on the phone, others with radios in their hands, and still more were pouring over maps.

"What's going on?" she demanded, dropping her bags and rushing over to the table where she knew Hassan, the lead guard, was on the phone. "Is it Jahlil? Is he okay?"

A split second later, everyone in the room froze, turning to stare at her.

"Maya!" Jahlil's deep voice shattered the sudden silence.

Maya spun around, eyes wide as she blinked back panicked tears. "Jahlil!" she whispered, then raced across the room to throw herself into his arms. "You're okay!" she whispered, pressing herself tightly against him, needing to reassure herself that he was safe and healthy. His arms were around her as well and she felt his cheek briefly rest against the top of her head.

"What's going on?" she asked, looking up at him. "Everyone looks as if there's a crisis!"

"Where have you been?" he demanded, gripping her upper arms.

"Me?" she squeaked. "I've been..." she looked around to discover that all of the guards were staring at her. Some seemed annoyed. "I just went shopping!" she exclaimed. "I didn't bring enough clothes for the week, so I took a taxi and got some more clothes," she explained.

"Maya, you can't just leave like that!" he told her, an edge to his tone that she'd never heard before.

"I...can't?" She stepped back enough to peer up at him, still confused. "But...I go shopping whenever I need something. It's never been a problem before."

"You've never...!" he started, only to stop as he pulled her back into his arms, holding her tenderly as if she were something precious! "Just don't leave without a guard with you from now on, okay?" he asked, his voice rough with unexplainable emotions.

"I won't," she whispered, trying very hard not to react to his closeness. It felt so good, too good, to be in his arms like this. Closing her eyes, she breathed in his spicy, male scent, absorbing each shift of his muscles against her body, savoring them for the future. For the time when she'd never feel them again.

"Did you eat?" he finally asked.

Maya pulled back and shook her head. She also remembered the guards that had filled the room and looked around. They were gone!

When had they disappeared? And how had they all left so silently?

Maybe they hadn't been as silent as she'd thought. Maya knew that she was pretty focused on Jahlil whenever he was around. His presence tended to obliterate everything else.

"Um…I'm not really hungry."

He sighed, pulling back even more. "I'll order something. You need to eat."

Maya laughed, putting a hand on his arm. The touch stopped his momentum and his eyes slashed to her. For a brief moment, there was something in his eyes. Heat? Desire? Or was she only seeing what she wanted to see?

But before she could interpret the look, it was gone, replaced by the ever-so-polite expression that she hated.

"You didn't eat on the plane, Maya. And you just admitted that you didn't stop for lunch. Why don't I just order a snack and then we'll go to the main dining room for dinner?"

Only because she knew that this was important to him, Maya agreed. It was his way of making sure that she was healthy. "That would be nice. Thank you," she finally replied. And even as the words left her mouth, she saw the tension leave his shoulders. "And truly, I'm sorry about leaving the resort without telling anyone this afternoon. I didn't even know that I should have done so."

"You're right," he replied, pulling his phone out of his pocket. While he typed a message, he continued, "No one informed you that this week might have…" he stopped typing on his phone and looked at her, his gaze guarded, "extra tension due to the meetings."

She stepped forward, her heart suddenly pounding. "Is it dangerous, Jahlil?" she asked, her lips feeling numb.

He paused and that was all the answer she needed. "Can you tell me what's going on? You look as if you could use someone to help brain-storm."

Jahlil watched Maya's features soften into an expression of concern and he ached to pull her back into his arms, to kiss her and make love to her. Then lay in bed, completely naked while he told her everything that was going on. These meetings were unprecedented. Danger lurked around every corner and he wondered if it had been a mistake to bring her here. Maybe she'd be safer back in Boston? But he hadn't been able to resist inviting her to stay with him. He knew that Maya loved sunshine and warmth.

Why she continued living in Boston was a mystery to him. She hated the cold weather. Every time he flew into the city to check in with her, she complained about the miserable snow, sleet, and the traffic that seemed to happen at all times of the day and night. The city had undergone "The Big Dig" several years ago, a massive construction project that created tunnels underneath the sky rise buildings, creating an interconnecting road system. The idea was to alleviate traffic congestion. But as was the case in so many of these "wonderful" endeavors, by the time the project was finished, it was completely inadequate to the new, higher needs of the city.

"Perhaps we could talk over dinner," he offered. "I should be in a meeting right now. I've ordered some food for you and it should arrive any minute. Will you be okay for a couple hours?"

Maya's eyes stopped glittering and he could see the hurt from his rejection in her eyes. And yet, she nodded politely. "Yes. Of course. Go do your thing," she said in that impertinent tone he loved.

Jahlil smiled at her jab, warmed that she still felt comfortable enough around him to do so. "I'll be back as soon as I can. The dining room is semi-formal here," he called out as he walked away from the one woman who never failed to touch his soul with her kindness and humor.

As he left, he wanted to punch something, anything to alleviate this building frustration. He didn't want to go to this damn meeting! He wanted to stay here and make sure that Maya ate something. He wanted to talk with her and tease her until she smiled. He wanted to take that pain out of her eyes. The pain that had been there ever since Sandoor....

Damn his brother for dying! As he walked towards the conference room, he cursed his brother a million times for doing something stupid which took his life and caused such pain in Maya. Even after five years, Jahlil knew that she still grieved for Sandoor. For the wonderful, fun-loving idiot who had earned her love.

Stepping into the conference room, he noticed the other two men already there, waiting for him. "I apologize for the delay," he said to the others, taking his seat around the circular table.

"Is your friend okay?" Zahir el Hassan, Sheik of Brumadi, asked, taking his own seat. Tazir el Moussa, ruler of Dilaar looked concerned as well. Their expressions, either fake or real, eased some of the tension that had been building since this morning.

"She's fine. She left to go shopping without a bodyguard. She didn't know that..." he stopped, not wanting to speak the words.

But Zahir, the big brute, had no problem putting it out there. "She didn't know that we're here and that we're working on a peace agreement that others might not want to happen," he finished.

Jahlil chuckled. "Well put," he confirmed.

Zahir smiled, shuffling the papers in front of him. "Perhaps we should hurry this process along. The faster we figure out the terms, the less time our enemies have to discover our efforts and stop us." He eyed the other two men. "It seems as if we all have...personal priorities that we'd like to protect."

Jahlil blinked at the man curiously. He'd seen Zahir with a woman yesterday, a beautiful woman with long, dark, flowing hair. Was he in the same situation? And Tazir...what was going on with him? Who was the little boy that had raced across the sand to him last night?

Yes, Jahlil suspected all three of them had similar agendas, none of which coincided with the efforts in this conference room. Which was good, he thought as he leaned forward, ready to dig into the tough issues. Knowing that these men were experiencing the same kind of problems gave him hope that they wouldn't hurt Maya. Mutually assured destruction, so to speak.

As the conversations continued, Jahlil was pleasantly surprised to find that all of them seemed to be much more open to compromise. And yet, his thoughts lingered around Maya. Was she eating the snack he'd ordered for her? Was she okay? Had he scared her earlier when he'd impressed upon her the urgency of taking a bodyguard with her wherever she went? He hadn't specified that she needed to do that even when she moved about the resort. But he'd mention it tonight over dinner.

And that caused him to wonder what she would wear to dinner tonight. Maya always looked beautiful. He loved sitting across the table from her and just looking at her. Her dark hair and crystal blue eyes calmed him in ways he didn't fully understand. Unfortunately, it was becoming harder to control his lust for her delectable body. She'd grown up over the past five years. Her maturity had only added to her beauty, giving her features depth and character. And her eyes! Damn, her blue eyes made him ache to see them filled with desire! For him!

He had to keep reminding himself that she was still grieving for Sandoor. Their love must have been amazing for her to still think of him, even after all this time. Yes, Jahlil missed his brother. The year after his passing had been the hardest.

How could he help Maya move on? How could he help her find love? Yes, he'd hoped that she might have feelings for him. But that wasn't going to happen. Maya had fallen in love with Sandoor, the fun, gregarious man-boy who could make riding the subway into an adventure. Maya didn't need someone like him. Jahlil knew that he was serious and sedate. He wasn't the kind of man that Maya could ever love.

Chapter 9

Maya smoothed the black fabric over her hips, wondering if it was too much. The simple dress had looked perfect on the hangar at one of the shops. She'd thought that it would be perfect for dinner tonight, so she'd hurriedly bought it, thinking she could return it if it didn't fit.

But now, looking at herself in the mirror, she thought that it was a mistake. The neckline was too low, showing off a significant amount of her cleavage. More than she'd ever revealed before! And the hemline was just a bit...well, higher than she was used to.

"I can't wear this!" she whispered. "It makes me look as if I'm trying to get Jahlil's attention!" She shifted in the mirror, looking at her butt. "I should wear something else."

"I think you look perfect!" Jahlil argued from behind her.

Maya swung around, startled to find him in her doorway. "Jahlil!" she gasped, stepping backwards slightly. "I didn't know that you'd finished your meeting!"

"We finished over an hour ago," he replied, stepping into the room. "And you shouldn't change. That dress looks incredible on you." He extended his arm to her. "Shall we go down to dinner?"

Maya stared at his arm, worried about touching him. After this afternoon, she wasn't sure she could handle being around Jahlil. And in this dress? Good grief, she looked like...she wasn't sure. Because she'd never dressed like this before.

"I should change," she repeated weakly.

"Nonsense," he argued, taking her hand and placing it on his arm. "You look spectacular."

Maya flushed with pleasure at his words. He might be lying, only being polite, but at this moment, she didn't care. "Thank you," she replied, walking beside him as he led her through the suite. His body guards circled them as the elevator doors opened. Maya had always wondered what it would be like to be Jahlil. He was constantly surrounded by people, guards, reporters, servants, staff…he rarely had a moment to himself. And yet, he also had every wish immediately catered to.

She noticed the tight set of his jaw and the intensity in his eyes. "Are you okay?" she asked.

She felt his other hand cover hers where it rested on his elbow. "With you here, I feel very honored."

She knew that wasn't an answer, but Maya also understood that he wouldn't tell her if something was wrong. He couldn't, she knew. Saying anything might endanger too many people.

"You have so much responsibility resting on your shoulders," she whispered, moving closer and leaning her head against his shoulder. "I'm sorry, Jahlil."

At Maya's touch, Jahlil experienced a surge of lust, but also a sense of rightness, of comfort. She understood. Too many women thought that he lived the life of luxury. But Maya understood what his life was *really* like. She grasped the enormous responsibility and the complexity of issues he had to resolve every day.

Plus, she was sensitive enough to understand that he couldn't talk about those problems. He wanted to. But he couldn't do that to her, nor could he violate security protocols by discussing the issues.

If she were his wife…!

Jahlil dismissed the idea as soon as it popped into his head. She wasn't his wife. She was still in love with Sandoor.

The doors to the elevator opened and the soft noise of the lobby enveloped them. He walked out, slowing his steps because Maya was in heels and…damn, those shoes made her legs look spectacular. Not that her legs didn't look lovely all the time! But in those heels…! He wanted to see her in those shoes…and nothing else! He wanted to feel her legs wrapped around his waist as he entered her, sliding into her heat and…!

Stop it, he snapped to himself.

"Your Highness," the maître d said as soon as he stepped into the elegant dining room. "Your table is this way."

As Jahlil moved through the tables, he noticed Tazir dining with the lovely brunette and…and the same little boy that he'd seen on the beach. The child looked startlingly similar to the arrogant ass. Even the boy's body language was similar. Tazir had a son?! That was definitely news!

Keeping his eyes forward, he moved to the table, holding Maya's chair as she sat down before taking his own seat.

As he spread the napkin over his lap, his eyes caught the low neckline of Maya's dress. Correction, he didn't give a damn about the neckline. He absolutely loved what that low neckline revealed! Normally, Maya wore sweaters or conservative outfits. This little, black dress was...hot!

"Jahlil?" Maya prompted.

Pulling his gaze away from those beautiful breasts, he looked at the sommelier, who was standing next to the table. "Might I recommend the Fitzaner white tonight?" he offered, referencing one of the new white wines that had hit the market with a buzz last year.

"That's fine," Jahlil snapped, trying to regain control over the sudden wave of lust. Unfortunately, Maya leaned forward, saying something about...hell, he had no idea. His eyes and his mind were too focused on that lovely cleavage. He thought about her nipples. He remembered seeing them that first night after Sandoor had brought her to Celina to meet him. They'd been mere shadows behind the worn tee shirt she'd donned for bed. But he'd easily discerned that her nipples were pink.

Pink nipples. His favorite. Okay, that was a lie, he thought, pulling his eyes away and trying to focus on the menu. He had no preference in the color of a woman's nipples. He just loved nipples! Well, the whole breast, but nipples were incredibly sexy. Big. Small. Tan, pink, mauve...he didn't care. He loved breasts!

He smiled to himself, wondering what Maya would say if she could read his thoughts. She'd probably stand up, slap him across the face, and stomp out in a huff!

Maya felt as if her whole body was on fire. Every time Jahlil looked at her, his eyes dropped to her chest. No, not her chest. He was staring at her breasts! It was the first time he'd ever looked at her like she was a woman! Her heart soared with hope!

Would it be horrible if she leaned forward, so that he got a better view? What if she revealed a bit more? Yes! Yes, that would be ridiculous. And crude! And yet, perhaps she could excuse herself, walk to the bathroom and shift her dress so that it was ever-so-slightly more revealing?

Maya silently laughed at herself. What was she thinking? Jahlil thought of her as a sister. A little sister, at that!

Instead of going to the restroom and readjusting her dress, Maya smiled across the table at him, reveling in her newfound power as a woman. A woman that Jahlil acknowledged. Oh, this dress had been the best investment she'd ever made!

The sommelier returned with the wine, doing the whole tasting ritual before pouring it. Maya watched, fascinated as Jahlil took a sip of the white wine, her eyes focused on his lips, wondering, not for the first time, what it would be like to be kissed by Jahlil. They talked about their trips and the weather, her job and the latest horses that were for sale around the world. They discussed world politics for a brief moment, but she quickly changed the subject to something more benign, sensing that Jahlil was uncomfortable, concerned about revealing something he shouldn't.

The wine was...wet. Maya ordered food and she might have eaten some of it, but by the time the waiter took her plate away, she couldn't say what she'd eaten. Chicken maybe? It had been white. But that might have been a cream sauce.

"Would you care to see the dessert menu?" the waiter offered, extending a small, elegant menu board to each of them.

Maya shook her head. "No, I don't think I could eat anything else." She smiled at the waiter. "Thank you though. Everything was delicious."

The waiter bowed away from the table and she turned back to Jahlil. "Thank you for dinner," she said softly.

"It was my pleasure," he replied easily. "Would you like to dance?"

Maya turned to look at the couples dancing in the distance. A small band played and a majority of the couples were older, so they mostly just swayed to the beat of the music.

"No, I don't think so," she told him honestly. "I think I'm a bit tired after traveling today."

"Of course," he said, and stood up, politely extending his hand to her. She took it, shivering as his strong fingers closed over her hand.

"Are you cold?" he asked, gallantly slipping his jacket off and draping it over her shoulders.

Cold? She felt as if she was on fire! She didn't want his coat, she thought. She wanted his arms! She wanted his whole body touching her! But instead, she satisfied herself with snuggling into the warmth left over from his body heat. And the jacket still held the scent of his aftershave. And him! Goodness, his scent was intoxicating! She wished she could bathe in it, revel in every part of him!

Instead, she walked beside him, the guards again surrounding them as they walked out of the restaurant and stepped back into the waiting elevator. It seemed as if his guards moved with a bit more...assertiveness than normal.

"Is something wrong?" she asked, stepping closer to his side.

"Why do you ask?" he asked, his arm wrapping around her waist.

Maya shrugged. "I don't know. There's just so much tension in the air." She watched his features carefully and saw the exact moment that he decided to lie to her.

"Everything is fine," he said.

She knew that wasn't true. But she also knew that he wasn't being honest because he was trying to protect her. Just as she'd done on the way down to the dining room, she leaned her head against his shoulder. "I wish that you wouldn't do that," she murmured.

"What's that?"

"Hide the truth from me," she said, her voice soft, non-accusatory. "I'm not a child, Jahlil." She huffed a bit, then pulled away from him. "I can handle whatever is going on." The doors to the elevator opened and she walked into the suite ahead of him. "You don't need to protect me from the truth." With that, she slipped out of his jacket and laid it carefully on the back of the sofa. "Thank you for dinner." And then she walked into her bedroom, softly closing the door. Instead of slamming it, as she desperately wanted to. She wanted to scream and throw a fit. She wanted to rush back out into the living room and pound on his chest with her fists until he acknowledged that she wasn't a child that he needed to protect.

Until he noticed her! She wanted him to acknowledge that she was a woman! A woman with a woman's needs and desires!

But she couldn't do that. She knew that Jahlil had a lot going on right now. He definitely didn't need a temperamental female putting additional burdens on his shoulders.

In the bathroom, she stripped off the dress, wishing she could wad it up and throw it away. Instead, she carefully hung it up in the closet, furious with herself for hoping that Jahlil might see her as a woman instead of a child.

Jahlil sipped his scotch, welcoming the burn as it slid down his throat. Tonight had been...both a disaster and a revelation. He ached to hold Maya in his arms, to kiss and make love to her, to discover every one of the secrets her body held, to learn everything that could make her cry out with pleasure.

And yet, she'd retreated from him. He'd probably offended her by staring at her in that stunning dress. He'd treated her badly and he'd have to apologize tomorrow.

Downing his scotch, he poured himself another, contemplating tomorrow when he'd get to sit across from her at breakfast. And yes, he knew that he'd get to share at least one more meal with her. Maybe more if he could apologize prettily enough to soothe her temper over tonight's lapse in manners. Maya always woke up in time to share breakfast with him, so at least he'd have that.

It wasn't much of a consolation, but it was something.

He had no idea how long he'd been sitting here, but he heard the door open and turned his head. The suite was dark, the only light coming from the moonlight shining off of the ocean and sifting through the windows onto the white furniture.

It wasn't a surprise when Maya padded out of her bedroom, heading for the kitchen. Milk, he thought. She was going to warm up some milk. She was having trouble sleeping again.

Even as he thought it, she reached for a glass.

"Need some help?" he asked, standing up.

She gasped and spun around. The sound of glass shattering broke the quiet of the night.

"Don't move!" he ordered, already knowing that she wasn't wearing shoes. Maya didn't like slippers, except during the winters. And even then, she usually wore thick socks. She'd always said that she liked to feel where she was going and shoes got in the way.

"I didn't realize that you were out here," she gasped, looking around at the floor. Glass was everywhere.

"I apologize for startling you." He moved swiftly across the suite. "Just stay there and I'll find a broom."

He dove into a small cupboard and came out with a broom and dustpan. She laughed, wondering how he even knew how to sweep.

"Are you sure you know how to use that?" she asked archly.

He looked at her, the light from the moon making her glow. He could see the teasing in her eyes and relief surged through him.

"I think I can figure it out," he shot back, a mocking tone to his voice now. "Just don't move."

Quickly, he swept the shards of glass up, sweeping everything into the dustpan, then dumping it all into the trash bin.

"How did you even know where those things are?" she asked, stepping away from the counter.

"Stop!" he ordered, lifting his hand. "There could still be bits I can't see."

Maya stood still as he leaned the broom and dustpan against the wall.

"How am I going to...?" She stopped when he bent down and scooped her up into his arms, her feet flying into the air. "Oh!" Maya yelped as she wrapped her arms around his neck. "Well, that's one way to deal with it!"

"You don't weigh enough, Maya," he grumbled, carrying her into the living room. He turned his head, looking into her eyes. In that moment, whatever teasing admonishment he might have uttered dried up.

The look in her eyes, the way her lips softened as she looked at him... everything disappeared in that instant.

In its place was desire. Hot, heavy, painful desire! Jahlil had never experienced desire like this before. Yes, he'd wanted Maya as his own from the very first moment he'd laid eyes on her. But he'd controlled that desire over the years.

Until now.

At this moment, as her body slid down against his as he released her legs, he couldn't have stopped the kiss from happening. Not even an explosion could have stopped him as he lowered his head. Maya could have stopped him, he supposed, but her fingers curled into the material of his shirt, pulling him down even as he lowered his head.

At the first brush of his lips against hers, desire flamed white hot, nearly blinding him. He lifted his head, looking down at her to see if she was offended. But her eyes were closed, her lips soft and slightly open, as if waiting for another kiss.

Because he was a gentleman, he kissed her again. And again. Every time, the kiss deepened until he was ravishing her mouth, his tongue mating with hers, doing all the things that his body wanted to do.

Groaning, he pulled her against his throbbing heat, needing to feel all of her against him. She gasped, but when he would have pulled away, she shivered, pressing closer in a way that he understood.

Mindless now, he lifted her back into his arms, but his gentlemanly instincts vaporized under the heat of his passion. This was raw lust. He cradled her bottom in his palms, pulling her more fully against his aching erection. His last ounce of propriety was used up as he carried her into his bedroom.

Once the door was closed, he moved quickly, stripping off her clothes. He wasn't aware of her pulling at his own clothes, but moments before he tumbled her back onto the bed, he found, with relief, that they were both naked!

"Tell me to stop!" he groaned, pinning her hands above her head, lacing his fingers through hers.

"Please don't stop!" she sobbed, wrapping her legs around his waist, exactly as he'd imagined so many times. But the reality was one hundred percent better!

His eyes moved lower and he wished that the lights were on so that he could properly see her breasts and her nipples. But he managed, finding them with his mouth as she arched into him. Sucking and teasing, he tortured one breast until she screamed. Smiling through the lust, he moved to the other, not stopping until she ripped her hands from his and pulled his head away. For a brief moment, he thought she was asking him to stop. But then her hands guided him back to the first breast and his relief was so intense, all thoughts vanished from his mind. Not that there were many anyway. Not with the way she tasted and the way his hands filled with the softness of those breasts.

He should be more reverent, perhaps. But her thighs rubbed against his hips and he abandoned her lovely breasts and those delicious nipples to explore his way down her amazing body. He kissed his way lower, moving over the soft curve of her stomach, smiling when she giggled when he found a ticklish spot. Then he kissed that spot again before moving lower. When he smelled her arousal, he almost surged back up so that he could thrust into her. But this was Maya! He needed all of her! He needed to know the taste of her.

Moving lower still, he breathed in the heat and scent a brief moment before his mouth moved closer. Just a small taste at first. But she was too delicious and he was a glutton. His mouth covered her, teasing that nub with his lips while his tongue explored her core, lapping at every delicious drop of her arousal. Needing to hear her scream, needing proof that she was with him, he latched onto that small nub, sucking and teasing, then sucking again until...his hands wrapped around her hips as she ground herself against his mouth, her body throbbing with an intense release that he could literally feel with his hands!

It was the most erotic moment of his life. Before her body could come down off of that climax, he lifted himself up and thrust into her! She was so wet, so hot and shockingly tight, he had to close his eyes as... thrusting harder, he froze! She was a virgin?!

Looking down at her, he noticed a tear escape from her eye and his body ached, but for a different reason now.

"I'm sorry, Maya!" he groaned, bending to kiss that tear away. "I'm so sorry!"

"Please, don't stop!" she begged, wrapping her arms around his neck as she lifted her hips, pressing against him. "Please, you feel so wonderful and I've waited so long for this. I don't want you to stop!"

Jahlil was humbled by this utterly unexpected gift. She hadn't ever been with Sandoor. She was all his!

Slowly, he started moving inside of her. Gentle now, he shifted ever so slightly, easing himself out of her tight sheath before moving slowly back into her.

"Faster?" she pleaded, then bit her lip in that delicious way.

Jahlil was more than happy to comply. Thrusting faster, but still as gently as his clamoring lust would allow, he moved deeper into her. Cradling Maya with his arms, he used every ounce of his expertise to bring her closer and closer to that blissful release again. Ignoring the desperate need for his own climax, he focused on ensuring that she found her pleasure. And when her body arched, her mouth opening as a silent scream left her, he felt her inner muscles clench spasmodically around his shaft.

Jahlil was able to hold out for another moment, but she felt too incredible, too tight and perfect. His own orgasm was a rush, draining everything out of him as he thrust into her faster and faster. Vaguely, he knew that she shivered once again with another, smaller climax coming over her. She wrapped her arms around his neck, pulling him close as she sighed with happiness.

A long time later, Jahlil lifted his head, looking down into her lovely features. She was beaming and relief surged through him. "Are you okay?" he asked, running a finger down over her features.

She laughed, arching her back ever so slightly. It was enough. His body hardened and her eyes widened. Her laugh was a delight to his ears and he kissed her lingeringly. Amazed, he started thrusting, trying to ease the desperate need in him. He suspected that Maya would be too tender for another round immediately, but her fingers slid into his hair and she lifted her head to kiss him, her hips lifting to match his thrusts.

When he tried to pull away, her legs tightened around his waist, holding him in place. "Don't go," she pleaded, her eyes closed as she rolled her hips.

After that, he was lost in the haze of lust, unable to unwind enough to give her a moment's peace. She was just that perfect, that gloriously sensual.

But Jahlil was also determined to make this time even better. Pulling back, he pressed his thumb against that nub, shifting so that every one of his thrusts brought her closer to that beautiful peak. Again and again, he listened to her soft sighs, her cries until he found the exact, right position. And then he thrust faster and faster, bringing her closer to that pleasure. When she cried out, he absorbed the sound into his mouth as he kissed her, his mouth and tongue mimicking his shaft as he feasted upon her.

Chapter 10

Maya woke up to the feeling that something was very different. First of all, she was lying on her stomach. She never slept on her stomach! She was a side sleeper, pulling her pillow in close and hugging it throughout the night.

Sunlight? What in the world? Her bedroom was dark. It was winter in Boston.

Then the previous day, and the long, sensuous night, came rushing back to her. Slowly, her confusion shifted to delight. She'd made love with Jahlil! After so many years of yearning for him to realize that she was a woman, that she...loved him, she finally knew what it was like to feel his passion. She knew what it was like to be a woman in Jahlil's arms.

Sitting up, she looked around. The bed was a mess! The pillows were scattered across the floor. Vaguely, she remembered resting her head on his chest as she fell into a deep, exhausted sleep. Maya couldn't remember sleeping so well in...well, ever! She pushed her hair out of her face, impressed at the tangles that probably looked like a rat's nest at this point.

"Goodness," she whispered into the morning sunshine.

Eagerly, she pushed the sheets away and headed into the bathroom, marveling at her sore muscles. There was a bit of unexpected tenderness in odd parts of her body as well, but she ignored that. "Nothing that a hot shower can't fix," she whispered, then gasped when she saw her image in the bathroom mirror. Her cheeks were red from Jahlil's rough beard, her hair was indeed going in every direction, and her lips were swollen.

Regardless, Maya felt...blissful! Is this what good sex did to one's psyche? If she'd known that, she might have...?

"No," she whispered, stepping into the shower and turning on the warm water. "It was Jahlil," she said out loud.

A long, hot shower revived her. Unfortunately, it didn't do much for her fear of facing Jahlil after last night. But seriously, why would she be nervous? He'd done things to her last night and...well, she'd touched him in ways that made her cheeks turn pink, but everything had been amazingly wonderful!

In other words, she shouldn't be embarrassed or nervous.

After pulling on a pair of shorts and a tee shirt, she stepped out of her bedroom, needing to face Jahlil and get the first "morning after" awkwardness out of the way.

Moving towards the living room, she half hoped that he'd already left for his meetings. But the clock showed that it was still relatively early. Jahlil generally ate breakfast around now.

Sure enough, as soon as she stepped out of the hallway, she spotted him sitting on the wide veranda, reading a newspaper and eating breakfast. Actually, he was only sipping coffee. No breakfast had been delivered yet.

Jahlil felt Maya's presence before he saw her. Turning his head, he watched as she approached the table and the elation that he'd felt last night and this morning upon waking with her in his arms, dissipated at the wary look in her eyes.

Standing up, he waited for her to come forward. "Good morning," he said, bowing slightly. She deserved his respect, at a minimum.

"Good morning," she replied, smiling tentatively.

"Are you hungry?"

She glanced at the table that held only his coffee cup. But as soon as the words left his mouth, a servant came forward, placing a mug in front of the other chair, as well as a plate and some muffins and biscuits with soft butter in a basket.

"Goodness, I'm always amazed at the service around you," she teased, taking the seat on the opposite side of the shaded table from him.

"Would you like something else?" he inquired, his movements stiff and formal.

Had she only imagined the passion in those dark eyes last night? Maya hesitated before sitting down. "Are you in a rush this morning?" she asked. "I can–"

"No," he interrupted, waiting until she was seated before taking his own chair. "No, we need to talk." He sighed and stood once more, moving to the bannister of the balcony, gripping the railing as he stared out at the ocean.

This wasn't good, Maya thought, pulling the linen napkin nervously over her lap. She bowed her head, her fingers twisting the edges of the napkin under the table. "Okay. Let's talk." About last night, she thought. "Obviously, you're going to–"

"I didn't use protection last night," he interrupted.

For a long moment, Maya merely blinked at him. She looked into his eyes, her heart sinking as she saw the regret in those dark depths. No protection. Um...well....

Maya sat very still, letting his words sink into her brain. Okay, that definitely wasn't where she'd thought this conversation was going! For a brief moment, relief surged through her. He hadn't told her last night had been a mistake! In her mind, it had been the most glorious night of her life. But at his formal attitude this morning, she'd feared that he'd regretted their night together.

Granted, he wasn't telling her that he loved what they'd done last night. But...he wasn't saying that it was a mistake! That gave her a small glimmer of hope.

He'd forgotten to use protection. The words echoed through her mind over and over again. They didn't make sense because she'd been ex-pecting something entirely different.

No protection. That meant...no condom. Um...Oh. *Oh!* "What?" she gasped, finally understanding. "You didn't...!" She stopped since he'd just answered it. "I'm um...I'm," she ran a hand through her hair, lean-ing her elbows on the table as the reality of the situation hit her. "I'm not on birth control," she whispered through numb lips.

"I suspected as much," he replied and his tone lifted her eyes towards him.

"I'm sorry." Maya said the words, but...deep down inside of her, she wasn't sorry at all! Good grief, how horrible was that? She wasn't sorry that there was the potential of a baby! Jahlil's baby! Her eyes actually welled up at the thought that she might be growing their child in her womb right now! The thought made her weak. And so happy, she was almost blinded by the possibility.

Pregnant! With Jahlil's child! With *their* child! A precious life that she could cherish for the rest of her life. If she couldn't have the man, she wanted their child!

"Um...well..." Maya gave up, not sure what to say. There were options. She could take a pill, but...no. She wasn't going to suggest that option. She wanted this child more than she'd ever wanted anything in her life! Okay, not as much as she wanted Jahlil in her life, for the rest of her life, but...*a baby!*

"We will need to marry at once," Jahlil announced, breaking through the blissfully happy dreams currently dancing through her mind. Dreams about giving birth and adoring this baby, giving this baby all of the love she'd kept hidden from Jahlil. All the love he didn't want!

But once again, he'd spoken words that didn't make sense. Marry. Marry? "We need to...what?" she asked, still blissfully making plans. Plans involving moving to a new city. One where this baby would have room to grow and run and learn without the pressures of city life and traffic and the pollutants that always came with a heavily populated area. She worked from home. Her online business meant that she could live anywhere!

"Yes. We must marry. Quickly and quietly. If you *are* pregnant, then there can be no doubt about the legitimacy of this child's right to rule after me."

Rule after him? "No!" she gasped, horrified at the thought of Jahlil dying! No, that simply couldn't happen. Standing up, she walked over to the balcony. "You're not going to die!" she whispered.

He stared down at her, that quirky-serious smile on his handsome features. "I don't intend to die anytime soon," he assured her, cupping her cheek in his palm. But he must have realized what he was doing and pulled away before she could fully absorb the warmth of his touch. "But the realities of my world include constant threats, Maya. You know this. It is why I am so heavily guarded all the time. It's why I was so worried when we couldn't find you yesterday." He sighed, rubbing a hand across the back of his neck. "My assistant will arrange a quiet, private wedding here at the resort. I'm so sorry, Maya," he said gently. "I know that this isn't the way you'd planned to be married, but it must happen." He turned, looking out at the ocean. "If it turns out that you are not pregnant, then we can quietly divorce. But until we know for sure..." he let the sentence linger in the air between them.

Maya's heart wasn't sure if it should soar with happiness at the suggested marriage or twist in pain at the idea of a divorce. Turning, she mimicked his stance, looking out at the ocean. But like him, she didn't see the beauty in front of her. Instead, her mind was working, trying to figure out what she needed to do. How could she make this man love her, even a little? If she were pregnant, would he love her a little? Could he learn to love her?

What if she wasn't pregnant? What if last night hadn't created a new life inside of her?

Closing her eyes, she prayed that a miracle had happened.

Jahlil turned, looking down at Maya. She'd been so quiet this morning. If she'd shown him even a small bit of joy over what had trans-pired last night, he might have kissed her. Hell, he might have tried to convince her to go right back into the bedroom and do all it all over again! Even now, looking at her in the cute shorts and stretchy top, he wanted to rip her clothes off and make love to her right here, under the blazing sun.

Last night had been too dark. He wanted to see what he'd been feeling and tasting! He wanted...hell, he wanted Maya!

And yet, she looked devastated at the thought of marrying him. How could so many other women desire him, and yet, the one woman he wanted more than anything in this world, didn't want him at all!

But...she'd wanted him last night. Had she been faking her passion? No, that was a ridiculous question. There was no way to fake that kind of a sexual response.

So...if she hadn't been faking it, what would she do if he kissed her right now?

Taking her hands, he turned her so that they were facing each other. "Is the thought of being married to me so horrifying, Maya?" he asked gently, heart in his throat.

"No!" she gasped, looking up at him. He felt her fingers curl around his hands, almost as if she needed to feel him just as much as he needed to touch her. "Not at all!"

"Was last night a trial for you?"

Maya laughed. "A trial?" Then her face softened. "Jahlil, last night was..." she paused. "It was beautiful. I've never felt anything like that before." Her lashes lowered and she sighed slightly. "I'm probably not supposed to say things like this, but last night was...unbelievably won-derful!" she finally finished, then peeked up at him through her lashes.

Jahlil looked into her eyes, trying to determine if she was just telling him what he wanted to hear. But there was genuine sincerity in her gaze. He kissed her before the thought finished forming. It was just a brief brush of his lips against hers. But because he was still holding her hands, he felt her shiver. Deciding that was good, especially since she inched closer, pulling her hands out of his light grasp and placing her hands on his chest, he did it again. And again! Deepening the kiss each time until he couldn't stand it any longer. He pulled her into his arms, pressing her softness against his body, trying to control the lust that was overwhelming his good sense.

A not-so-subtle cough interrupted their moment. As Jahlil straight-ened up, he was ready to fire whoever had interrupted this interlude.

Unfortunately, duty was an always-present monster. Slowly, he released Maya and turned, finding Ormond in the doorway. "Yes?" he snapped, more harshly than he'd meant to speak.

Ormond cringed slightly. "My apologies for interrupting, Your Highness. Your next meeting is in five minutes."

Jahlil sighed, but he nodded. "I'll be there. Give me a moment."

Ormond nodded, bowing as he left the terrace.

Jahlil turned to Maya. Putting a hand to her cheek, he looked into her eyes. "I'm sorry about this plan. But it has to be this way. Can you be ready tonight?" he asked.

"Absolutely," she told him. "Don't worry about me, Jahlil. I'm fine." She gave him a tentative smile and a slight shrug. "Go to your meetings."

He wanted to stay here and talk to her, to figure out what was going through her mind. But these meetings were beyond important. He couldn't be late. So, instead of kissing her like he wanted, he pressed a gentle kiss to her forehead, then stepped back. "If you wouldn't mind, could you stay here in the resort where my guards can protect you?"

"Absolutely," she replied immediately, smiling in response. "I won't disappear again."

"Thank you," he said, relief surging through him. "Until tonight then."

"Good luck," she called after him.

He kept walking, fighting the urge to look back over his shoulder as he went.

Chapter 11

Maya sipped the hot, fragrant coffee, going through everything that had just happened. She was marrying Jahlil. Because there was a potential baby. Because of last night's incredible passion!

Married! She was to *marry* Jahlil! Her deepest secret longings were about to become a reality!

When she stared into the dark liquid, she thought about the potential for a child. What would she do with a sweet, adorable baby? Love them, obviously. Teach them how to be a responsible, compassionate, generous person, she thought.

Dirty diapers. Sleepless nights. The fears and anxieties about caring for a child...yes, she knew about those issues. Maya had enough friends who had already gone through childbirth to know that pregnancy wasn't always the blissful, wonderful forty weeks that the baby food commercials portrayed. It could sometimes be a living nightmare. But she also knew from her friends that those nightmarish moments were compensated for by bursts of pure joy and happiness.

Something occurred to her as she looked down at her cup. Coffee. Coffee? She couldn't drink coffee! If she was pregnant, then she couldn't have caffeine.

Carefully setting the delicate cup down into the saucer, she looked around. Instantly, a servant appeared. "How can I help you, ma'am?" he asked, bowing ever so slightly.

"Could I have a cup of herbal tea?" she asked.

The man bowed in reply. "Of course. I'll get it for you right away. Is there anything else you'd like for breakfast?"

Maya thought about that for a moment. Usually, she didn't eat breakfast. She just woke up, went for a run, showered and worked from the home office she'd set up. But, if she was pregnant, then her baby would need better nutrition. She couldn't skip meals like she had in the past.

"How about a bowl of fresh fruit?" she asked.

"Absolutely, ma'am. Anything else?"

Maya couldn't think about what else a growing baby might need. She'd have to read up about it. "No, that's all for now. Thank you very much."

The man bowed again, then left the terrace. Maya had seen the subservience of the staff at the palace in Celina towards Jahlil and found it annoying. But she hadn't ever been subjected to this kind of deference. Now she knew that it was a pain in the butt!

Ormond stepped onto the terrace. "Ma'am, I apologize for interrupting your breakfast, but His Highness asked that I procure a special dress for you." He tapped on his tablet, then looked at her. "Would you mind telling me your size?"

Maya was a bit startled. She hadn't gotten as far as the logistics of marrying a man by the end of the day. But obviously, Jahlil had. He'd gone so far as to tell his personal assistant to get the event organized. Good grief!

She frowned thoughtfully up at Ormond. "A dress!" she repeated, sitting up straighter as she thought about it. "I guess I'm a size eight or ten?"

The man bowed, and typed something into his tablet. "Excellent. And do you have a preference on dinner tonight?"

Preference on dinner. Interesting thought. "I guess some sort of chicken and a variety of vegetables," she told him, once again thinking about her baby.

"I'll make that happen," he replied, backing away, still tapping on that tablet. She had no idea what that guy was typing, but she suspected that it was a whole lot more than just her dress size and meal preference.

Taking a deep breath, she contemplated her existence today compared to yesterday. Everything looked different now, simply because last night had changed...everything! She might be pregnant. She was getting married to the man she'd been madly in love with for five years. She was on a beautiful tropical island instead of back in snowy Boston. What more could a woman want?

Maybe the assurance that the man she was marrying loved her back. And the knowledge that she wouldn't be forced into a divorce if she wasn't pregnant.

Chapter 12

Maya sighed as she flipped through the pages of her book. She'd already read this one. Why had she brought it again?

Her gaze lifted, drifting to the large, elegant cabana set up on the far side of the pool. Three men sat around a small table, serious and concerned about whatever it was they were discussing.

Jahlil was one of them. She hadn't meant to interrupt his concentration, but she knew that he looked over at her occasionally. The black, two piece bathing suit she was wearing wasn't particularly revealing. It was actually pretty conservative, compared to some of the other bathing suits she'd seen women wearing. But still, every time she caught Jahlil looking at her, she felt...naked. Was he undressing her with his eyes?

Wishful thinking, she decided. Jahlil was one of the most focused men she'd ever met. He'd never mentally undress a woman while he was working. And besides, she was too far away. He probably didn't even recognize her from this distance.

Another woman, a lovely brunette, walked over to the cabana. She looked irritated about something, but Maya had no idea what and she was too far away to overhear the conversation. But one of the men from the cabana stood up and kissed her. It was a searing kiss, even from this distance. But the man stepped away from her, moving back to his chair inside the cabana.

The woman looked around, then wandered in a seemingly aimless manner around the pool. She looked angry, and Maya wondered why.

It appeared as if she might just leave the pool area. It was very crowded. In fact, the only empty chaise lounge was the one next to Maya. And that chair was being guarded by the big, scary men behind her. As soon as the woman's eyes lit upon the empty chaise, Maya gave her a welcoming smile, gesturing towards the chair.

The woman looked intensely relieved as she walked over to the chair and sat down. Well, she flopped into the chair, obviously flustered.

"Your husband is very sweet," Maya commented.

The lovely woman turned her head. "I'm sorry?"

Maya nodded towards the three men in the cabana. "Sheik el Moussa," she clarified, recognizing the other two leaders because of the research she'd done after acknowledging her feelings for Jahlil. "Of those three, he's probably the kindest," she continued.

The woman looked stunned. "You know him?"

Maya shrugged, flipping the page in her book. "I recognize all three of them." She looked at the men again, thinking of the conversation with Jahlil this morning. "One of them is my fiancé," she admitted. That word sent a thrill of pleasure throughout her whole body. "I'm Maya Tisdale," she said to the pretty woman. "And you are?"

"Brielle Capson," the other woman replied, looking over at the men.

"Your son is adorable," Maya replied, thinking of the little boy she'd seen in the dining room last night. He looked exactly like his dad. Even from a distance, she could see the resemblance.

"Thank you," Brielle smiled, her shoulders relaxing as she thought about her son. "Which one is your fiancé?"

"He's the one sitting next to your husband." She sighed, looking down at her book. "I'm not even sure that he knows that I'm here."

Brielle blinked, her golden eyes reminding Maya of a lion. "I'm sure he's–"

Maya shook her head. "Our relationship is…complicated," she said.

After that, they talked of other things and the time passed wonderfully. Fruity drinks were delivered, as were a variety of snacks. Maya wondered if Jahlil had ordered them because he discovered that she'd only eaten fruit for breakfast, but she didn't mind. She was hungry and the ever present possibility of a baby kept her focused on nutrition.

About mid-afternoon, Maya waved goodbye to the other woman, thinking she was a very nice person. She'd love to get to know Brielle a bit better, but they'd probably never see each other again after today. Still, it had been nice to talk with someone. Being with Jahlil tended to be a bit…isolating. She'd never considered it before, but with his security detail so close by, she didn't feel as if she could converse with just anyone.

After washing off the sunscreen, Maya changed and stepped out of her bedroom, only to find Ormond standing there in the great room, waiting for her. "Oh!" she gasped, startled by his presence.

"My apologies Ms. Tisdale," he said, bowing slightly. "His Highness asked that I arrange for some wedding dresses for you to choose from." He waved towards a rack that had been rolled into the room. "I called several designers here on the island and was able to procure ten of them for your review." He stepped back. "Choose whichever you prefer and I'll arrange to have the others returned."

Maya was impressed by his efficiency. And even more astounded by the selection of dresses. There were full ball gowns, which would flare out into a massive skirt, as well as silky, slinky gowns that would skim over her figure.

Carefully, she walked over to the rack, letting her fingers skim down over the elegant dresses. "This is..." She stopped, overwhelmed and speechless. That seemed to be happening to her a lot today. Normally, Maya considered herself to be a rather articulate person. But when Jahlil was involved, her brain literally fizzled and, too often, she found herself stammering out replies that didn't always make sense.

This was one of those situations. Admiring the beautiful wedding dresses, she wasn't sure what to say or think.

"When is the wedding going to take place?" she asked, pulling her hand away.

Ormond glanced at his tablet. "His Highness has a break between meetings at five thirty, Ms. Tisdale," he recited easily.

Okay, that really hurt. Jahlil was going to fit their wedding into a handy moment between his meetings. Obviously, the event wasn't a huge concern for him. It was just another box to check on his list of activities for the day.

With that thought in mind, she sifted through the dresses and found the least formal of the batch. It was a white satin design that was a hybrid of a sundress and a sexy negligee. The trim was a bit thicker than what would be on a nightdress, but that was the only concession to real life.

As she picked it up, she surveyed the dress dispassionately. It would serve a dual purpose, she told herself. It was the most casual of the dresses, despite the satin, which subtly implied formality. But it was also decadently sexy. Not to mention, because of the low back, she couldn't wear a bra.

Hmm...maybe that was a mistake, she thought. Maya was just on the side of voluptuous where a dress like this, one that she couldn't wear a bra, might be *too* sexy.

And yet, maybe this dress was exactly what she needed! Perhaps the style of this dress, and her inability to wear a bra underneath, might stir Jahlil's lust and transform their wedding from just another meeting on his daily agenda into something more significant.

"I should probably try several of these on," she said to Ormond, who stood back, patiently waiting for her to make a decision.

"As you wish," the man said, doing that annoying bow-thing again. She glanced at him, but pressed her lips together.

He took the rack of dresses and pushed it into the bedroom she was using, Maya following behind. After he backed out of the room, pulling the door closed behind him, she banished him from her thoughts.

"A wedding dress," she muttered, running gentle fingers over the beautiful fabrics. "I'm to be married in a rushed ceremony that will be shoehorned between meetings." She sighed heavily. "Every woman's dream wedding."

With resignation, Maya turned to look through the other dresses. There were tea-length dresses and ball gowns, evening gowns and even one demure suit. She pulled that one out, thinking that she should probably wear it. And yet, her eyes kept returning to the satin shift.

In the end, she lifted it off the rack and held it up to her figure, looking at herself in the mirror. "Do I dare?" she whispered to her reflection in the mirror. Biting her lip, she shifted to the right and left. "You're always so cautious! Why not be daring?" she asked herself. "It's about time that you reached out and grabbed your dreams!"

And with that thought in mind, she made her decision!

Laying the dress on the bed, she went into the bathroom to shower. She buffed and scrubbed, then used her vanilla body lotion to soften her skin. Afterwards, she curled her hair and pulled it up into a loose style on top of her head. The overall look was sexy and yet, somehow demure. "I like it!" she beamed at her reflection in the mirror.

Afterwards, she slipped the dress over her head, letting it slide down her body. Sure enough, a bra wouldn't work. So she reached behind her back and slipped the bra off. With relish, she noticed that her nipples were visible, pressing against the white satin. "Perfect!" she decided. If she was going to get married, then she wanted Jahlil to notice her. Plus, she wanted a wedding night!

She didn't have shoes, she realized. Looking at the rack again, she discovered that there were shoes on a hidden lower shelf and she found a pair of strappy sandals that were pretty painful to wear, but as soon as she slipped them onto her feet, Maya knew that they were perfect! First of all, they gave her an extra three inches of height. Plus, they made her legs look awesome!

"Are you ready, Ms. Tisdale?" Ormond asked after knocking on the door.

Maya looked at her image in the mirror. Her makeup was soft and subtle, her hair looked amazing on top of her head with light tendrils gracing her neck. She wasn't wearing earrings, because she didn't have anything that would work with something this dramatic.

Stepping out into the great room, she looked around. "Where is Jahlil?" The air conditioning made her shiver. Or perhaps it was the anticipation of seeing Jahlil.

"He will meet you at the ceremony," Ormond replied, not looking up from his tablet. "If you are ready," he prompted, waving towards the doorway.

"Of course," Maya replied, reaching behind her and lifting the small train of her dress so it didn't drag along the floor.

As soon as she stepped into the elevator, Maya found herself surrounded by bodyguards. This was very odd, she thought. But again, it wasn't all that different from what Jahlil endured every day. Still, she glanced up at the men out of the corner of her eye, warily wondering how long this level of protection would last.

Thankfully, the elevator doors opened and Maya literally burst through them, feeling a bit claustrophobic in the very full elevator.

"This way, Ms. Tisdale," Ormond explained, gesturing towards a sidewalk of the resort she hadn't noticed before.

"What's this way?"

Ormond did his little bowing gesture as he explained, "His Highness is waiting for you on the beach for the ceremony."

Beach? How...romantic! But Jahlil wasn't a romantic sort of guy! He was sensible and responsible. He was unbelievably patient, but also demanding. He demanded results from his staff and got it. At least, that's what Sandoor had always said. She'd seen Jahlil in action many times over the years, despite Jahlil's efforts to keep business to a minimum during their sporadic dinners together.

Still, she walked down the sidewalk, wondering what she would find.

As she rounded the corner, Maya stopped and gasped. A beautiful, flowered archway had been placed in the sand. Standing just behind the archway was a minister, waiting patiently. And to the right was Jahlil. He looked...magnificent! His white linen shirt and tan linen slacks billowed in the soft breeze coming off of the ocean. And yet, despite his casual clothes, he looked elegant and powerful. He literally took her breath away as he stood waiting for her to arrive. Impatiently, she realized, as he glanced at his watch.

And yet, in that same moment, he looked up and froze when he spotted her.

That movement, plus the look in his eyes, gave her the boost of confidence that she desperately needed.

"Ms. Tisdale?" a female voice interrupted her moment.

Maya looked around to find a pretty woman with a gamin smile. "Yes?"

The woman's smile widened. "Flowers for you," she said, handing Maya a beautiful bouquet of tropical flowers surrounded by dark, green leaves and wrapped with a silk ribbon. The flowers perfectly matched the flowers on the archway.

The ocean, the sand, the flowers, and...and Jahlil. Each part came together to make this moment perfect. Stepping down the stone steps, she felt her heart swell.

At least, she hoped that she was special to him. She *wanted* to be special to him.

His eyes glowed as he watched her walk down the aisle to his side. Taking the bouquet from her, he tossed the flowers to someone off to the side, then took both of her hands in his, lifting them to his lips. Gently, he kissed each one and, in that moment, she felt as if he were promising her something much more precious than any vows.

The minister began to speak but Maya was only vaguely aware of him. She was focused on Jahlil. The skin over his cheekbones was tight, as if he were clenching his teeth. Because he didn't want this? Just as that thought flashed through her, his fingers tightened around hers. It was as if he were sending her a silent signal, a message that he wanted more.

This was so confusing. But, she stopped trying to figure it out, and simply enjoyed the fact that she was marrying Jahlil, the man she'd loved for so long! She didn't care if she was pregnant. She was marrying Jahlil. The marriage might only last for a couple of weeks, but it would be the best two weeks of her life, Maya vowed!

And then he kissed her! Had they said their vows? Maya didn't remember. But she'd remember his kiss forever! The sensation of his lips on hers, his hands pulling her in close as his hard muscles pressed against her, was like a clap of thunder – startling and unnerving. Maya didn't pull away though. She pressed even closer. She remembered the previous night and wanted that. She wanted it all, but she'd settle for these shockingly beautiful moments.

Jahlil pulled away, aware of the fact that he was starting to lose control.

He swallowed a chuckle at the thought. Starting? He'd lost control long ago when it came to Maya. With the culmination of that loss of control last night and continuing when he'd seen her in this dress. The satin shimmered over her soft, beautiful curves, showing him everything! As soon as he'd seen her, Jahlil was glad that this was a private ceremony. Now, he wanted a private dinner. Correction, he wanted a private bedroom, where he could let his hands explore every inch of her body in that stunning, shimmering gown that was the epitome of sin laced with beautiful sensuality.

"Are we married?" she whispered, her lips swollen from the power of that kiss.

He laughed softly, his fingers caressing her trim waist. "Yes. We're married."

"Good," she whispered back, licking her lips, which caused his lust to explode into an inferno!

"Are you hungry?"

She beamed. "Famished!"

The look in her eyes warned him that it wasn't food she wanted. She wanted...him! Damn, he couldn't believe this was happening!

He took her hand and led her back up the beach and the stairs. When she moved too slowly, he bent and scooped her up. He needed her. And he really couldn't wait much longer!

The guards had the elevator doors open and he stepped in, growling with impatience.

"You can put me down now," she whispered in his ear as her fingers moved into his hair and he almost dropped her.

"Only for a moment," he replied, releasing her legs, but keeping an arm around her. When she stood again, he pulled her close, but didn't kiss her. Not in front of his guards. He knew that Maya was shy around others and he didn't want to embarrass her.

Thankfully, the elevator doors opened and he took her hand, pausing only long enough to allow her to gather the bottom of her dress before he almost dragged her into the suite.

"Now, about this dress," he murmured as he pulled her into his bedroom. He spun her around and she landed against his chest.

Laughing, she leaned into him. "I thought you'd like this dress," she replied, her voice huskier than normal.

He cupped her bottom, before letting his hands slide upwards. "I love the dress," he murmured, lowering his head to kiss her softly. But as his hands slid over her body, he couldn't slow down. Not with her looking like this and feeling so soft and perfect against him! His kiss deepened and he lifted her up, laying her down on the bed. He pulled her dress straps down, revealing what he'd already suspected. She wasn't wearing a bra! Damn, but he loved the way she looked right at this moment!

"I need you now, Jahlil!" she whispered, fumbling with the buttons on his shirt.

With a frustrated growl, he stood up and literally ripped his clothes off, tossing them away. He didn't want anything between himself and Maya!

When he was naked, he moved back to the bed. She'd watched him the whole time, her mouth slightly open. That was a heady sensation. After years of trying to view her as a younger sister, it was shocking how badly he needed to treat her as he really viewed her; as a lover.

"You're not naked," he commented, and was proud that his voice didn't sound as raw as he felt.

"I just..." she trailed off, her eyes drifting closed as his hands slid up her calves, shifting the satin out of the way. He stared down at his hands as they revealed her delicate, pale skin. She was so damn beautiful! Her legs were strong and muscular because she loved to run in the mornings. And her skin was so soft and beautiful, he wanted to touch and feel and taste every inch of her!

"This is even better," he told her, his eyes following the path of his hands as he revealed more of her lovely skin. "I'll treat you like a present, mine to unwrap."

She smiled and his hands moved higher. The smile disappeared, replaced with that soft, melting need in her eyes. He liked that look. It turned him on, made him hotter. He ached with the desperate need to bury himself in her heat. He should slow down, he thought. Maya might be tender from their first night together, so he was determined to take it slow this time. And he'd use protection. They hadn't talked about the consequences of last night since this morning, except for the fact that they were now married. He had to take this slow and protect her, just in case she wasn't pregnant.

Then he caught sight of her panties. What little there was of them. His mind blanked and, with a tug, they were gone, revealing the lush pink folds that so entranced him.

"Jahlil," she whispered as he spread her legs wider. He paused, taking in the whole picture. Her legs looked longer than ever in her pretty heels. The satin dress bunched around her waist, her breasts free with their pink tips hard and waiting for him. Every part of her seemed to glisten with arousal and passion. Bending, he lowered his head to lap at that sensitive nub. But that small taste wasn't enough! He needed more. One finger slid into her soft, tight sheath as his mouth closed over that sensitive nub. Sucking and teasing, he felt her body moving in time with his mouth. It wasn't enough. He needed her complete and total surrender as well as more of those soft, sweet sounds that she made in the back of her throat!

It didn't take long before she cried out, her body shimmering with her exultant release and he laughed, feeling more powerful with that small cry than he'd ever felt in his life!

But then he looked up the line of her body and saw her back arching, it was just too much for him. He lifted himself higher and pressed into her heat, grabbing her hands so that he could pull them over her head. Thrusting slowly, he drove into her again and again, feeling her body arch into his, feeling her shivers from that first orgasm start to fade, just as her body tightened, ready for more.

Moving faster, he pressed into her, shifting his body the way he remembered she'd liked last night. Over and over, he thrust into her, her cries of delight making his mind spin out of control. Gritting his teeth, he held on until...she screamed his name. Then he let go, pressing into her heat again and again as his own climax nearly blinded him. The pleasure was so intense, he was lost in it, and he prayed that he didn't hurt Maya with the overwhelming lust as his body drained into hers.

Chapter 13

Maya's eyes fluttered open and she smiled as the watery, morning sunshine filtered into the room. Unlike yesterday morning, Jahlil was still with her. His muscular arms surrounded her and he held her tightly against him. For a moment, she snuggled up against him, absorbing the warmth from his body and hearing his heart beat.

Last night, her wedding night, had been amazing. Over and over again, Jahlil had made love to her. She'd been so overwhelmed with passion that she hadn't been able to move when he'd finally turned out the light. They'd slept in each other's arms for a while, but one of them would wake up and start it all over again. She'd loved every moment of it, wishing that she could love Jahlil like that forever.

They hadn't had dinner last night, she realized as her stomach growled. Turning her head, she gazed up at Jahlil's sleeping face. His jawline was dark from the night's growth of his beard. In the dim light, she noticed his lashes were longer than she'd realized, like lace across his cheekbones. And in sleep, he was just as ruggedly handsome as he was during his waking hours. There was no relaxation of his features. It was almost as if he was still going through all of the weighty issues that he faced during the day, even in his sleep.

Maya couldn't help but smile. He was so strong, so responsible, and... and they hadn't used protection during that first round last night. He'd apologized again, but Maya had only smiled, kissed his chest, and the whole whirlwind had started all over again.

She loved him. It was an almost overwhelming feeling, loving Jahlil. It was going to be painful to leave him. But she knew this marriage was only temporary. He'd said so himself. If she wasn't pregnant, then they'd divorce.

With that in mind, she slipped out of bed and into her own bedroom.

There, she showered and pulled on a pair of shorts and a tee-shirt. She knew what she had to do. Leave. She had to get back to her life. Back to the real world and her routines. If she found that she was pregnant, then she'd let Jahlil know immediately. Pulling out her phone, she searched through the flight information until she came up with a plan. Because of the remoteness of the island, there wasn't a direct flight to Boston. It would take a while to get home, since she'd need to get a short flight from here to Belize, then another flight from Belize to Houston. From Houston, she could catch a flight to Boston. Good grief, that was going to be a long day of traveling, but she'd get there. Eventually.

Sitting down at the small, hotel desk, she wrote him a note. And this time, she didn't leave anything out. She told him everything, wiping away tears as she wrote. After the past two nights, she couldn't hold anything back. He'd given her so much. Jahlil deserved to know why she was leaving and why she couldn't stay with him.

When she was done, she folded it up and wrote his name on the outside, then propped it up on the bed.

After packing up the few clothes she'd brought with her, she quietly stepped out of the beautiful suite without a backwards glance.

Jahlil woke with a start. Something was wrong. Rubbing his face, he looked around, trying to figure out why he felt this intense sensation of doom. The shimmering dress that Maya had worn for their wedding was still on the floor, partially covered by his own clothes. They probably should have picked those up, but Jahlil hadn't been able to stop touching her. She'd been softer than he'd thought possible, and more responsive than any lover he'd ever been with.

That's when he realized what was so wrong. Maya wasn't in his bed. The bright, Caribbean sunshine streamed in through the huge windows of the master bedroom. The ocean continued to roll against the shoreline, there were birds chirping in the mango tree that grew up outside of his window. It was a normal day. Another day without Maya, he thought with a sigh. He would have loved to wake up with her in his arms, but she was an early riser. She was probably out on a run, he thought. He hoped that she'd remembered to tell her guards.

Staring up at the ceiling, he thought through his schedule, wondering if there'd be time to take Maya on an excursion somewhere on the island. Unfortunately, he had yet another day filled with tedious meetings and tense negotiations. Slumping back against the pillow, he wondered if he could just tell the others that he agreed with all of their proposals just so that he could spirit Maya away, spend some private time with her.

But he couldn't. He knew that the negotiations were going extremely well and if he didn't hurry, he'd be late. Blowing off the meetings simply wasn't an option.

Muttering curses, he stepped into the shower, wishing that Maya was still with him. He'd like to shower with her, to make sure that she wasn't sore from the passion with which he'd made love to her last night. It seemed that every time they were together, he lost control and needed her to do the same. Was it because he needed to somehow mark her as his own?

He smiled at the thought. Yes, he definitely wanted to claim her as his own. But the ring on her finger proved that point perfectly. She was his. She was his *wife*! Damn, that sounded so right! For too many years, he'd longed for her to be his, and now the reality was so much better than any of his fantasies!

Glancing at the time, he muttered several expletives. He was going to be late if he didn't hurry. So much for checking in with Maya, and maybe having breakfast with her. She must have gone for a long run, he thought.

Two hours later, the group finally took a break. Jahlil stood up, turning to talk to his guards, needing to know what Maya had for breakfast and what she was up to. He felt a stab of guilt for abandoning her on what was essentially their honeymoon.

Before he could signal one of his guards for information, Zahir came up to him, extending his hand with a warm smile. "I understand that congratulations are in order."

Jahlil was surprised he even knew about his wedding yesterday. Then again, he had his men watching the other two leaders, wanting to know what was going on. It made sense that Zahir and Tazir were doing the same thing.

He smiled politely, taking the other man's hand. "Yes. I married a woman I've known for about five years," he said, and Tazir turned startled eyes towards them as well. They were walking towards the pool area now and it was just as crowded as yesterday.

"That's wonderful!" Zahir replied, turning to glance over his shoulder. Was he watching the delightful woman leading a line of small children through the pool area?

"Congratulations!" Tazir said as well, balancing the coffee cup and saucer in one hand while he shook Jahlil's hand with the other. "How did you make that happen?"

Jahlil walked over to the coffee cart as well, pouring a cup for himself. "The resort arranged everything," he said, adding cream. "They did an exceptional job." When he turned back, Tazir was staring at a woman reading a book on the far side of the pool. Was that...? Jahlil once again turned to look at Zahir. Sure enough, he was rubbing his mouth while still staring at the woman with the children.

Zahir pulled his eyes away as the adorable woman with the children disappeared around the corner, politely smiling as he came back to the present and nodded to Jahlil. "This is excellent news," the leader replied in a tone that wasn't mocking, as Jahlil had expected. The man was renowned for his mistresses, each more beautiful than the last. So why was he watching a beautiful resort employee? The woman was lovely but...well, Jahlil was just confused.

"I congratulate you on your wedding," Zahir said. "Perhaps it is time to follow in your path and do the same." His eyes glanced quickly towards the now empty space, then back to Jahlil. "Now that we're making our region a safer place, we should find good women to share our lives with."

The man turned, looking at Tazir. "Your son is a handsome and energetic boy. I hope to have such luck in the future."

Tazir chuckled. "Yes, my son will be a very handsome fellow," he agreed.

Jahlil remembered the boy who had looked startlingly similar to the ruler of Dilaar. But to admit that he had a son so openly? That was something that Jahlil craved as well. Not just one child though. No, he wanted a large family. He craved children! That was a startling thought, since he hadn't ever really considered children before. But now that he was married, as well as the possibility that Maya was pregnant, the idea seemed to gnaw at his soul. He'd wanted Maya for so long, and now, to have her as well as a possible child?

He shook his head as he contemplated a future with Maya. Looking around, he wondered again what she was doing. He half expected her to come down to the pool in that black bathing suit again. Well, he *hoped* she'd come down again.

Pulling out his phone, he texted Ormond, asking him to check on her and make sure that she had everything she needed.

The group came back together, tossing around ideas for the peace treaty. The conversations were significantly more productive than Jahlil had anticipated. What's more, he was growing to respect these men. He didn't consider them to be friends. That was a bit much and he doubted that he'd ever reach that level of trust with them. But he wasn't as suspicious about their motives now. Trust was building with each concession.

Still, he looked around, wondering where Maya had gone.

At that same moment, he watched as Ormond hurried along the edge of the pool, carefully side stepping the other guests who were enjoying their vacations in the sunshine.

Something about the way that his assistant moved, or perhaps it was the nervous expression in his eyes, warned Jahlil that something was wrong.

Sure enough, Ormond stepped into the cabana, his eyes darting to the other two men with an anxious expression. "Your Highness, I apologize for the interruption." He bowed before handing a note to Jahlil.

Something warned him that he wasn't going to like whatever was in that note. He took it anyway, noticing that the envelope only had his name on the outside. Okay, that was good, he thought. It wasn't a military issue. If it had been a military problem, then it wouldn't have Maya's beautiful script on the outside.

Tearing open the envelope, he pulled out the paper, absently noting that it was a letter written on the resort's letterhead. Jahlil read the words written in Maya's sweet style, but every muscle in his body tightened with dread. Before he'd gotten through the first paragraph, his mind froze and he couldn't make sense of the words.

Dear Jahlil, I apologize for writing instead of having the courage to tell you in person. First, let me say that the previous two nights changed my life and I will treasure them in my heart forever! But because of my feelings for you, I have to go. I'm heading back to Boston and...

She'd left the island! Maya was in danger! Damn it, she had no idea of the danger she was in.

"I believe there is a problem," Zahir stated, concern in his eyes as Jahlil crumpled the letter, then immediately flattened it back out. The other two men stood up, clearly alarmed. "Go, Jahlil. Whatever it is, it must be seen to. We'll stop here and resume at a later date." The man turned, glancing at Tazir for confirmation. "I believe we've made significant progress here. I, for one, would like to continue this conversation but," he nodded to Jahlil, "after our friend has resolved whatever problem has arisen." He smiled slightly. "I believe that we are all struggling to keep our attention on the tedious issues here when," he laughed softly, "we have such lovely ladies we'd rather focus on."

Jahlil vaguely noticed their gentle chuckles.

"I suggest we resume next week. Does that give everyone enough time to resolve our personal issues?"

Jahlil nodded sharply, then squeezed Zahir's shoulder. "Thank you for understanding," he said. Without another word, he hurried away, only slightly relieved that they wanted to focus on their women as well. For him, this was a question of national security! Maya had left the resort without her security detail! She was alone, out in the world, without protection!

Damn it, he should have explained more carefully the need to inform her bodyguards about her actions! But he hadn't wanted to scare her. She'd gone from being just a regular person one day to a member of the royal family the next!

Perhaps she had been lulled into a false sense of security because Jahlil hadn't bothered with his guards most of the time while here on the resort. Or at least, it appeared that he wasn't informing them of his plans. What she didn't know was that they were always there, in the background. His schedule was carefully monitored and his guards scoured the areas where Jahlil would be prior to his arrival.

He flashed back to her time with Sandoor, wondering if...it was possible. Sandoor had been pretty lax about informing his guards about his plans. No, they hadn't been able to protect Sandoor during the rock-climbing incident. But they'd been there. They'd gotten Sandoor to the hospital as quickly as possible. Unfortunately, that hadn't been enough to save him.

But Maya didn't know that. She only knew the fun-loving, spirited guy she'd fallen in...No! Correction. He smoothed out the letter, quickly skimming through Maya's words. Yes, she'd loved Sandoor but – and his heart soared as he read the rest of the note – she had never been *in love* with Sandoor! Those words thrilled him.

But the reality was Maya was his *wife*. That alone put her in danger! To make it worse, she also might be pregnant, and that made him feel sick as he thought about what his enemies could do with that information.

Ormond jogged to keep up, but didn't speak. They had worked so hard to keep this week's negotiations a secret from the world, but who knew what could happen? The world wasn't the friendly, wonderful place that so many people believed it to be. It was greedy, violent, and people got hurt all the time by nefarious actors trying to gain an advantage.

As soon as he stepped into the suite, he knew that his security team was working hard to locate her. There was a low level of chatter as his team worked to find out where she'd gone.

"I've found her!" someone called out, waving a hand in the air.

Over the next half hour, the team found the flight she'd boarded, but it was flying over Georgia at the moment. Jahlil sighed with relief, his body aching after the tension of the past hour. For now, Maya was safe. But the next step, intercepting her, was going to be even more challenging.

"She'll head to her house," Jahlil announced with absolute certainty.

"She won't go anywhere else." He rubbed a hand over his face, trying to shake off the wave of anxiety that threatened to engulf him. "She doesn't understand how important it is for her to be guarded," he told the security lead, needing to explain so that the security team wasn't angry with her. "This is all so new to her and she..." he sighed heavily, not sure how else to explain Maya's disappearance.

The head of his security team nodded brusquely, then spoke quietly into the microphone attached to his collar. The man nodded, then referred to the map, scribbling notations along the margins.

Jahlil paced back and forth, impatiently waiting for word that they'd secured Maya, or, at least, that they had a plan.

Chapter 14

Maya fought off a yawn as she walked off the plane. She'd been traveling for hours, and all she wanted to do was get home and curl up on her bed and cry. She desperately missed Jahlil and wished that she'd at least taken a moment to say goodbye to him instead of leaving that stupid note and running away. After all they'd been through over the past few days, he'd deserved that much, at least.

On the flight home, Maya made some decisions. She'd had long hours to figure things out and one thing was clear; she loved Jahlil and, she suspected that his feelings for her were stronger than she'd realized. He definitely didn't think of her as a little sister, or the fiancé to his baby brother. No, that assumption had gone out the window the day of their wedding. No man could make love to a woman as Jahlil had and think of her as a little sister.

So, Maya was going to fight for him. Somewhere over Tennessee or Kentucky, she'd decided that she was going to win Jahlil's love. He obviously desired her, so she was going to try to turn that lust into love. She was going to prove to him that she could be a good wife and a wonderful mother to his children. If she wasn't pregnant yet, she was going to ask him to keep trying.

Running a hand over her flat stomach, Maya smiled at the prospect.

With the question of Jahlil's feelings somewhat resolved, Maya wanted to figure out one more mystery. And there was only one person who could answer her question.

Since she only had one bag, Maya was able to walk out the doors of Logan Airport as soon as she landed in Boston and grab a taxi. She remembered the luxury of the town car that had driven her to the airport several days ago and sighed wistfully. Yeah, that had been pretty nice. Thankfully, there was a long line of taxis waiting for passengers. She smiled at the man who directed the line of taxis. "Just me and one bag," she told the man who immediately whistled, gesturing the next cab driver forward.

After stepping over the greyish sludge that was all that remained of the last snowfall, she settled into the back of the cab, rubbing her hands together in an effort to warm herself up. "Just a moment," she said to the taxi driver. She pulled her phone out of her purse, flipping through the contacts until she found the address she wanted. "Can you take me to…" and she gave him the street and building number, then sat back as the driver maneuvered around the other cars picking up passengers. As she sat there, she scanned the parking lot, looking at the exit. That's when she spotted the two men. These men stood at the exit where passengers hurried to waiting cars, taxis or crossing the street to reach the shuttle busses that would take them to the parking lots.

The two men didn't move, she thought, a feeling of unease crawling up her spine. They stood by the doors, glancing casually around as if they didn't have a care in the world. They had no luggage, so they weren't coming or going. And this area of the airport didn't encourage people to park and linger. It was too busy and the airport law enforcement agents were quick to shoo lingering vehicles away from the curb.

So, who were they? For some reason, her heart began pounding frantically against her ribs. Were they looking for her? No way! Maya told herself that the possibility was ridiculous. Jahlil was the only person who knew she was here! And he couldn't know that her plane had landed yet. Nor could he guess which taxi she'd gotten into!

Still, she sank lower in the back seat, not wanting the men to spot her. Maya waited anxiously as the cab driver honked, yelling at someone who cut him off.

Holding her breath, she watched as the men looked around, obviously searching for someone.

As soon as they passed by her, Maya scooted back up, peering out the passenger side window. They were probably looking for someone else, she told herself. This was a massive airport with thousands of people coming and going. The idea that two men were searching for her was silly!

Thankfully, the taxi driver finally found enough space to pull away from the curb. Since it was the middle of the afternoon getting through the traffic was easier than she'd anticipated. Perhaps the cab driver just knew all the best shortcuts to avoid traffic. When they reached the small apartment building she jumped out, paying and thanking the cab driver profusely. Pulling out her phone, she dialed the number, crossing her fingers that the number was still valid.

"Mike?" she asked as a male voice answered. "This is Maya. Maya Tisdale?" she prompted.

There was a moment's hesitation before he replied. "Yeah, hi Maya. How are you? How have you been?" Mike finally replied. The words were eager enough, but the tone indicated that Mike didn't sound very happy to hear from her.

"I was wondering if you might have a moment to talk to me."

"Sure," he replied. "How about next week?"

She laughed, thinking he was trying to put her off. "How about now? I'm outside your apartment complex. Any chance you have a minute right now?"

There was a long silence and she could picture him closing his eyes and pinching the bridge of his nose. Exactly how Sandoor used to. Those two were like peas in a pod.

After a heavy sigh, Mike finally replied, "Sure, Maya. Why not? Come on up."

His response was less than enthusiastic, but she tamped down her trepidation. She pressed the button for his apartment, and waited until he buzzed her inside.

After walking up the three flights of narrow stairs, she found Mike leaning in the open doorway to his apartment. "Come on in, Maya," he said, waving her inside.

Smiling, she pulled her pashmina off and shivered. "It's warm in here," she said, smiling shyly.

He took two mugs down from the shelf and poured coffee into both. "You look tan. Where have you been?"

Maya slipped onto one of the stools set up under the breakfast bar, wrapping her cold hands around the hot mug, trying to warm them up. "I just got back from a short trip to the Caribbean," she explained.

"Nice ring," he commented, tilting at her hand as he took a long sip of his coffee.

Maya glanced down at the diamond ring on her finger. It was far more understated than the ring Sandoor had given her so many years ago and she much preferred this one. It was still lovely, but not nearly as gaudy.

"Thank you." She took a deep breath, deciding to just ask her question. She was tired of wondering. "Would you tell me about your relationship with Sandoor, please?" she asked.

Mike stiffened. For a long moment, he stared down into the dark depths of his mug. Then he sighed and looked up. "We were friends," he said shortly, then turned his back to her, indicating that there was something he didn't want Maya to see.

"Mike," she started off, toying mindlessly with the mug, "there are a lot of things about five years ago that confuse me. But over the past few days, I've discovered that some of those assumptions about those years were false." She considered how to phrase her question. "Were you and Sandoor...in love?" she blurted out.

Mike spun around, eyes wide with surprise. "What the hell? You two were engaged! Shouldn't you know if Sandoor was gay?"

She smiled crookedly. "Yes I was, but we were never intimate." She considered her next words carefully. "In fact, Sandoor never even *really* kissed me."

Mike scoffed. "He was always touching you."

"Yes," she agreed, nodding her head. "Sandoor was an affectionate friend. But," she paused, looking directly at Mike, "that's *all* we were. We were friends." She paused again, then shrugged a shoulder. "I think he was in love with you."

Pain flashed across Mike's face and he bowed his head. For a long time, there was silence. Finally, Mike lifted his head and Maya noticed the tears in his eyes. "Yes. Sandoor and I were in love. I loved him... still love him, even now." He ruthlessly scrubbed the tears away. "I still haven't gotten over him." He took a deep breath. "But Sandoor needed to marry a woman. He couldn't be seen in his country as gay. They would have killed him for it. It's," his voice cracked. "It's illegal."

Maya felt the tears burn in her eyes. "So much pain," she whispered.

Mike walked over to the window, his coffee forgotten as he thought back to those years. "When you turned Sandoor down the first time, I begged him to stop asking you to marry him," Mike said, angry now. "But he kept trying to convince you. He said he had to. For his brother."

"He was wrong," Maya replied, trying to blink back the tears. But there were too many of them and they fell down her cheeks like rain. "Mike, I think that Sandoor loved you very much."

"He did!" Mike snapped. He bit back the angry words that had been on the tip of his tongue, his body almost vibrating. "But in the end, it wasn't enough! He didn't love me enough to tell his brother the truth."

"He was scared," she said gently. "We were just young, stupid kids thinking we were adults and understood the world." She stood up and walked over to Mike. "I'm sorry that I got in the way of your relationship. Is it any consolation that he never cheated on you with me?"

"No!" Mike replied. Then he closed his eyes and sighed, his shoulders sagging. "Yes!"

Maya laughed, but it sounded a bit damp. "I think I know what you're going through. I've loved a man for so long, but I thought that he only saw me as Sandoor's little sister."

"That bastard?" Mike snapped, turning to face her with a righteous fury in his eyes now. "You're in love with Jahlil? How *could* you?"

"Because he changed the laws, Mike," she whispered. "He'd changed the laws about gay relationships more than ten years ago, as soon as their father died. Sandoor didn't know, but the laws against homosexual relationships are long gone."

Mike's mouth fell open. "But...!"

"I know," she whispered. "I know that Sandoor didn't realize that. But I don't know if knowing would have changed anything. He still looked up to Jahlil so much." She laughed, but it came out harsh and brittle. "Trust me, Jahlil is a difficult man to disappoint!"

He snorted, and Maya realized that he agreed. "Sandoor loved his brother so much," he finally said.

Maya bowed her head. "Yeah. I know. But," she sighed and stood up, "Jahlil...I'm finding that it's hard not to love him. He's–"

"Don't!" Mike whispered, pain crackling through his voice now. "Just...." he stopped and shook his head.

"Thank you for being honest with me," she said, putting her untouched cup of coffee into the sink. "It clears up one of the mysteries."

"Happy to help," Mike said, sarcasm dripping from his tone.

She smiled, and touched his arm. "Sandoor was an amazing man. I hope that, eventually, you will be able to move on with your life."

Mike nodded, but there was still a lot of pain in his eyes. Maya moved to the door and pulled it open. "Good luck Mike," she said, then walked out. She didn't look back now, feeling...liberated. Sandoor hadn't loved her. At least, not in the way a man loves a woman. They'd only been good friends. That meant that her feelings for Jahlil weren't a betrayal.

Feeling the guilt lift from her, Maya crossed the parking lot to the subway station, smiling to herself. Yes, this was a good thing. She felt horrible for Mike. But Maya needed to release the past, release Sandoor, and embrace the future! She needed to grab it with both hands!

And the first thing she needed to do was to call Jahlil and tell him so! She'd said it in her note, but she needed to tell him in person. She owed him that.

With that in mind, she stepped onto the subway, making her way back to her apartment. It was slow going because the evening commuters were out in force. By the time she stepped out of the subway station near her building, she was more than ready to pack up her house and fly out to find Jahlil.

But as she reached her building, an ominous presence loomed over her.

"Where the hell have you been?" a deep, menacing voice demanded. At the same time, her upper arms were grabbed firmly and she was pulled against a hard, familiar chest.

"Jahlil?" she asked, terrified as she blinked into the dim light of the street light.

"Were you expecting someone else?" he growled.

There were more shadows surrounding them, causing her heart to hammer against her ribs. "Who are all these people?" she asked, pressing herself against the only person she knew was safe. Jahlil's arms wrapped around her, but for some reason, his touch felt different today.

"They are my guards," he snapped, then his arms tightened around her. "And yours, Maya! They are your guards! Damn it, how could you leave me a day after we were married?!"

She pulled back, pressing her hands against his chest. He didn't release her, but he gave her enough space to look up at him. "I explained in the note," she said, confused.

"You said you loved me!" he growled, his hands stroking her back. "And that's the only reason I'm not bending you over my knee and spanking your adorable ass!"

She laughed, warmed by his concern, even if it was a bit...okay, she kind of liked the idea. Not that she would tell him though!

"Jahlil, in the note, I mentioned that I needed to figure some things out."

He looked at her, his face shadowed from the descending night. "You said that you loved me. You said you needed to clear up some issues in order to be with me. But you didn't tell me what those issues might be."

She rested a hand against his chest. "I needed to get some more notes for work, Jahlil. I only planned to be away from my office and my clients for a couple days. And I needed more clothes. I'd planned to meet you in Celina, which I explained in the note."

He sighed, his forehead resting against hers. "You don't understand, Maya," he groaned.

She lifted up onto her toes. "Would you mind explaining what I don't understand?" she prompted, wrapping her arms around the back of his neck.

His fingers tightened on her arms. "I love you!" he whispered, as if it pained him to admit it. "I've loved you for so long!"

The beaming smile that washed over her features was like the sun coming out after a storm. "You...*do*?" she whispered.

"Yes!" he pulled her close. "I've loved you ever since the first moment I saw you, the day my brother brought you to meet me. But you were off limits."

She kissed him lingeringly. "I've felt the same way," she admitted. "But...Sandoor."

There was a long silence. "Yes. My brother." He took her hand and led her into her apartment. Inside, he looked around and a guard immediately stepped forward. He gave Jahlil a nod, then stepped out into the hallway.

"How long has that man been in my house?" she asked, peering through the windows at the courtyard below. She noticed several more guards tromping through the snow and ice, looking very intimidating. She wondered what her neighbors thought of all this, suspecting that some might call the police.

"Ever since I realized that you were gone," he explained. "But don't worry about the guards, Maya. Explain why you left me. Was it because of Sandoor? Is he always going to stand between us?"

She turned, startled. "NO! I *never* loved Sandoor," she said. "Not the way I should have."

His eyes narrowed and she felt his arms tighten. "But you came to Celina engaged to my brother."

She smiled, relieved that he was thinking back to the past five years as well. "I know," she replied, gesturing for him to sit down. He joined her on the small sofa. "The thing is, Sandoor had been trying to convince me to marry him for a while. I'd thought we were just friends. It all started one night over pizza, when he asked me to marry him out of the blue. I laughed, thinking that he was kidding." She grimaced. "He wasn't. He thought that we were compatible. When I pointed out that we were just friends, he argued that being friends first was a good thing. That we loved each other enough to build a strong marriage, together." She took his hand. "The thing is, Sandoor was gay," she told him, then held her breath, waiting for his reaction.

Jahlil nodded, rubbing his neck as he looked around the room. "I know."

"You *know*?" she parroted, startled by his reaction. "I mean...you're not angry?"

Jahlil laughed. "Of course I'm not angry. I've known Sandoor was gay since he was about five years old and he made our GI Joe dolls make out."

Maya stared at Jahlil for a long moment, then burst out laughing. "For so long, I've felt guilty for not loving Sandoor the way a fiancée should have. But when I started to think about it, I realized that he'd never touched me the way you did. He never even touched me the way he touched Mike. So..."

He'd been looking out the window, but with her admission, his head swung around, his eyes looking at her intently. "Is that where you've been?"

Maya smiled, nodding for emphasis. "Yes. I went straight to Mike's apartment after the airport. I knew that I wanted to pack up as many things as I could and come back to you. But I needed to know." She tightened her hands on Jahlil's. "Mike still thinks about Sandoor. He's still in love with your brother. Apparently, they were madly in love."

"That's how I feel about you, Maya," he said, and pulled her onto his lap. "I've lived without you for the past five years. I don't want to do it any longer." He kissed her and all of those passionate feelings welled up inside of her. She wrapped her arms around his neck, reveling in his kiss. When he finally lifted his head, he glared down at her. "But I swear, Maya, if you *ever* leave without your guards again, I'm going to spank you until you can't sit down!"

She stared blankly at him for a long moment. "Guards?"

"Yes, damn it!" he snapped, lifting her up and setting her back on the sofa. Jahlil stood up and started pacing, rubbing his forehead. "How can I get you to understand that you can't just go off on your own? You must tell your guards where you're going. In advance. You're my *wife* now! You must be protected!"

"But, Jahlil, I don't have–"

"You do now! From the moment I made love to you, you were my woman, Maya," he snapped, slicing his hand through the air. "You're mine and I won't let you go! And I *will* protect you from harm!"

She liked the sound of being his woman. It sounded...a bit sexist, but also extremely nice! "What does being your woman entail?" she asked, standing up and moving closer to him, a sultry look in her eyes.

He reached out automatically, resting his hands on her waist. "It means that I get to protect you."

"And?" she asked, fiddling with a button on his shirt.

"And you don't go *anywhere* without me or your guards."

"And?" she prompted again, her fingers sliding between the material to caress his chest. She felt the hiss of his breath and the tightening of his fingers around her waist.

"And...?" Her finger moved slightly.

"Oh Maya!" he groaned.

Maya licked her lips, pressing her soft curves against the hardness of his chest. "I want more than just your protection, Jahlil."

"What do you want?"

She smiled. "First, I want you to tell me again that you love me."

"I love you," he replied, his voice husky as he lowered his head.

"Then I want you to make love to me. As my husband."

He stilled. Maya had closed her eyes, anticipating the touch of his lips. But instead, he pulled back and...Maya shrieked with laughter as he tossed her over his shoulder. "Where's your bedroom, my woman?"

"Upstairs!" she announced, pointing the way. "But wouldn't it be faster if I walked?"

He swatted her bottom in response, which only made her laugh harder. In the back of her mind, Maya wondered if she should worry about the guards standing out in the cold. Their feet must be blocks of ice by now.

But then Jahlil kissed her.

Epilogue

Maya stepped out onto the balcony, squinting her eyes in the distance. Sure enough, Jahlil was racing along on his horse, tearing across the flat plains. Little puffs of dust spread out behind him as well as behind the smaller horse. For a long moment, Maya held her breath, watching as Jahlil and their seven year old daughter laughed, galloping together until they pulled their horses to a walk. Even from this distance, she could hear their laughter.

"I'm going to kill him!" Maya muttered, waddling past her guards who merely smiled at her threat to their illustrious leader. It wasn't the first time she'd uttered those words. But they all knew that she'd never hurt Jahlil.

Maya waddled down the wide stairs, ignoring the guards who walked closely beside her. She knew that they moved closer now, ready to catch her if she started to tilt off balance.

She wasn't in the mood to smile her thanks to her overly protective guards today. At this moment, she wanted to...she was going to...!

"Jahlil!" she yelled as soon as he and their daughter, Jayla, walked into the palace.

Jayla and Jahlil looked at each other, both of them silently cringing at her tone.

"You promised!" she snapped, coming to an awkward halt in front of the pair.

"I promised what?" he asked.

Maya looked at Jayla. "Your French tutor is waiting for you, honey. You'd better hurry up and change your clothes. You know how much your tutor hates the smell of horses."

Jayla grinned, eager to tease her tutor. "I do!" she said, then skipped away, flinging a wave goodbye to her parents.

Maya waited until Jayla and her personal guards were out of range before she turned to glare up at her husband. "You promised!" she hissed.

Jahlil moved closer, resting his hands on her round tummy. "What was this promise I gave you, love?" he asked gently, leaning closer to kiss her lips.

"You promised that we wouldn't have to host that stupid gala!" she hissed. "You know how much I hate Dilaar's ambassador! He's such a creep!"

Jahlil laughed and, because she'd turned her head, he moved his kissed to the side, nibbling on her neck. "Yes. But in this instance, the ambassador won't be coming. This will be for…"

Maya pushed away from him, her eyes turning from angry to…excited. "Are Tazir and Zahir coming?" she gasped.

"Yes, but…"

"That means that Andi and Brielle will be here as well, right?" she demanded, already turning around, grabbing Jahlil's hands as she waddled and tugged him towards their suite. "Oh, I can't wait to see them again."

Jahlil laughed, shaking his head. "You know, they used to be our enemies," he told her with a slight admonishment in his voice.

Maya waved her hand in the air dismissively. "Oh, don't you even try it! I know that the three of you sneak away from every official meeting and play cards or shoot pool!"

Jahlil couldn't argue with her there because she was right. The two men who used to be his most hated enemies had turned out to be his closest friends. And most of that had been brought about by Maya's friendships with the men's wives.

"Where are we going?" he asked, hoping that she was leading them to their bedroom. She looked especially beautiful in this blue, flowered dress that flowed over her softly rounded belly in a delicious fashion.

"Stop thinking that," Maya warned, laughing when he pulled her back around, right into his arms. "Have I mentioned that you're beautiful?"

Maya's surprise shifted into a happy glow. "No. Not today," she told him, sliding her hands up so that her fingers could loop around his neck.

"You are," he said, then kissed her softly.

"I love you," she whispered back.

"I love you too."

She smiled, thinking that she was the luckiest woman in the world!

Message from Elizabeth:
So how was it? Did you like this story?
Anyway, would you take just a few seconds to leave a review for Jahlil and Maya's story? Go back to the retail site's book page. Just a few words are extremely helpful! Thank you so much!
(If you don't want to leave feedback in a public forum, feel free to e-mail me directly at elizabeth@elizabethlennox.com. I answer all e-mails per-sonally, although it sometimes takes me a while. Please don't be offended if I don't respond immediately. I tend to lose myself in writing stories and have a hard time pulling my head out of the book.)

Keep scrolling for a sneak preview of "Claiming His Heir" – Tazir and Brielle's story! I hope that you enjoy it!

Excerpt to "Claiming His Heir"
Release Date: November 12, 2021

"Oomph!"

She opened her eyes and looked up as strong hands wrapped around her upper arms and a hard, rock-like chest pressed against her breasts. But when she focused, there wasn't a face in front of her. Instead, she saw only tanned skin and muscles. Lots of muscles!

The fingers that were wrapped around her arms tightened slightly as she lifted her eyes higher. But the image in front of her couldn't be right! She blinked, trying to re-focus her eyes, or get her brain back in gear. Because...it couldn't be! There was no way that...it couldn't be!

"Tazir!" she gasped. The man on the balcony! Broad shoulders, arrogant stance...her eyes hadn't been playing tricks on her! "It *was* you!"

Her fingers uncurled from fists, sliding over bare skin. Had he just come from swimming in the ocean? Goodness, his skin was so cold... and yet she could feel the heat from his muscles simmering below the surface. Unfortunately, warning bells blared in her mind.

"Brielle!" he groaned, shifting as a couple tried to pass them on the sidewalk. He moved so that they were off the pathway and...goodness, they were practically hidden by the lush vegetation! The sun no longer warmed her skin. Instead, it was Tazir that warmed her. She suddenly realized that they were touching from her breasts all the way down to her knees. She didn't care about the water seeping into her sundress because Tazir was holding her! She'd dreamed about this moment so many times over the last five years, never thinking to see him again!

"What are you doing here?" she asked in a whisper, afraid that anything louder might shatter this precious moment. It had happened so often in her dreams. She'd wake up from a beautiful dream, then his arms would vanish and her heart would shatter all over again.

For a brief moment, there was a reciprocal heat in his dark eyes and his hands tightened around her arms. She could feel his body's reaction and knew that there was something wrong there, but, she couldn't figure out why it was so wrong to feel so good.

"I have meetings," he told her. His answer was vague, as if he didn't want her to know anything more than just the superficial details. Just like old times, she thought.

"Well," she licked her lips, her eyes darting lower to stare at his mouth, but then she shifted. This wasn't right, she told herself. *Tazir* wasn't good for her. She'd spent the last five years trying to get over him. She couldn't, *wouldn't*, step right back into his arms and endure another cruel and unexplained disappearance. He'd disappear just like he'd done five years ago and Brielle didn't know if she could pick up the pieces again. "I have to go," she said. "It was nice seeing you again."

"Why?"

She flinched, stunned by the ferocity in his voice. But then she blinked, looking into his eyes and tried to understand what he was asking. "Why what?"

For a long moment, neither moved. She stared up at him, sensing his inner turmoil. Was that anger she felt from him? Slowly, her fingers curled away from his chest and she stepped back.

At the separation of their bodies, his features hardened into granite. "Nothing," he finally replied, releasing her arms and stepping back, giving her space. "You look good," he said softly.

"Thank you," Brielle replied, bowing her head slightly. Then she realized what she was doing and lifted her head, glaring at him. Reviving her self-esteem, she inhaled slowly and deeply, then let the breath out. When she looked up at him this time, she was more composed. With a firm nod, she said, "Have a nice day," then cautiously stepped around him, careful not to touch any part of him. Once had been enough.

With as much dignity as she could muster, Brielle walked down the sidewalk towards the...well, she wasn't sure where she was going. Just away. Away from Tazir. Away from the pain. Away from the betrayal and the memories.

Unfortunately, the confusing wash of horrid emotions followed her. But she couldn't do that again! She wasn't going to wallow in the misery any longer! She was over him! She was stronger now!

Instead of heading to her suite to hide for the rest of the day, Brielle walked into the open air dining room and asked for a cup of coffee. The waitress smiled and, a moment later, brought over an entire pot.

Brielle sat for a long moment, ignoring the books and magazines in her bag as she tried to come to terms with seeing Tazir again.

So, it *had* been him on the balcony last night. Brielle didn't like that Tazir was here at the same resort. But what could she do about it? She could leave, but Luke would be devastated and...!

Luke! Good grief, she hadn't even thought about Luke. She checked her watch and realized that she'd been sitting here for an hour.

But Luke was...Tazir's son! Five years ago, when she'd realized she was pregnant, Brielle hadn't known how to get in touch with Tazir. She'd gone over their conversations in her mind and realized she didn't even know his last name! They'd spent hours talking about politics and art, literature and their childhoods. But he'd never mentioned his last name. Or where he was from. She knew that he had two younger sisters, that he'd tormented them mercilessly over the years, and that they were married with children. But she didn't know *where* he'd tormented them. She knew that he wasn't from the United States. She knew that he spoke seven languages. But she'd had no way to tell him of her pregnancy since he'd blocked her text messages!

But now...now he was here. And Luke was here!